LAST TRAIN

Published by: Archer Quill Publishing
Cover Design : Stacker Designs
Editing by: Lexis Cummings @ Book and Mark It
Editing
Bookandmarkit.editing@gmail.com
ISBN: 978-1-956988-12-3 (Paperback)
ISBN: 978-1-956988-50-5 (Ebook)

Dedication:

To all of us who live
vicariously through
Rom-coms

Shout Out:

Congratulations to Miranda Kimball
for winning the "be in a book" contest!

With every book I publish, I pick a
winner to have their name in the next
book.
Go to
https://www.facebook.com/RomAuth
orDebbieMitchell/
To find out when the next contest is

Check out other books by this author:

The Unfortunate Souls MC series:
Benelli's Elle-Book One
(please see www.authordmitchell.com
for triggers) (Insta-love)
Stack'd Against Ruger-Book Two
(Friends to lovers/Second chance
romance)
Phoenix's Zen-Book Three (Insta-love)

Hot Cocoa & Shenanigans
(A sweet holiday novella)

The Biker's Baby
(It was just supposed to be a one-night
stand)

A Touch of Magic
(under Deb Mitchell)
(suitable for 12 & up)

Last Train
(enemies to lovers/rom-com)

Coming in 2023
Devil's Handmaidens MC -Mystic Bayou,
LA chapter
Right as Reign-Book One

CHAPTER ONE

It never fails. When I have an important meeting, something happens, and I run late. None of the software seems to be working, or there are compatibility issues. *Compatibility issues, ha. Isn't that the truth.* I haven't found anyone compatible in a very long time. Right now, though, it's getting my writing software to work with the new windows update that apparently happened as I slept.

After I spent the morning trying to stay calm, and "undo" the update, I ended up locking my laptop in the HP spinning death screen. *Don't panic*, I tell myself and pour me another cup of coffee. The bring-me-back-to-life brew filling my senses. A heaping spoonful of sugar, and a good swoosh of creamer. That's the stuff right there. Breakfast of champions. *I can do this*. Okay, I've Googled, and it says something about holding down the window icon and the letter "b". Now, the power button for two to three seconds. *Yes! Praise the goddess of laptops, it's working*. My writing software still isn't working, but I'm at least back in.

I've called and pushed the meeting back with the publisher till later. I've got a few hours to get this all sorted out. It probably wouldn't be such an issue if I would have just done the fancy new update, and learned it last year. Everyone in the ScribeIt world went on and on about how awesome it was going to be. I did the update and HATED it! Probably because it wasn't basically the same, and was a whole new learning curve. Deadlines needed to be met, and who has time for that. Not me. My latest romance novel needed to be sent to the editor immediately. The publish date was quickly arriving.

That's when I made the quick decision two months ago to go back to the old version, pressing forward. With a little tweaking, it made it to the editor and back. Now, the publisher has it. My newest tale is in his hands. So, why mess with perfection? I continued with the old version. That was, until this morning. I swear, my computer updating, and the fact I didn't update the writing software, have to be connected.

My warm mug between my palms, adorned with pictures of my covers from my romance series, I stare at the screen. *Okay, think.* I believe it's time to bite the bullet, and do the damn update. A big sip of the energizing, magical brew, and I click the download button. Here goes nothing. I can do this. It can't be that complicated, right? I know they can compile and save it as an Ebook. They are one of the big five publishing companies, after all. Call it being a temper-mental author. Indie was my jam back in the day, and I'm stuck in my ways. I want to know exactly what it's going to look like before it comes out.

Once I get passed all the extras, I see the manuscript icon, the chapters, the scenes. I rename things to what I'm accustomed to. I'm on my way. I go to the Ebook section and drop in my cover. *Success! I've got this.* I finish off the coffee, and set down my cup. On with the other story I've been working on. It is rapidly moving along, and before I even realize, I'm three chapters into my next novel. I'm what they call a pantser. Outlines, pish posh. Those things are used only in the event that I become stuck in the story. It's then I giggle at myself. *Pish, posh.* You would think I am writing a period piece.

Shoot! I look down at the time in the bottom, right corner. I swiftly hIt save, and just to be safe, do a quick compile, saving that, too. You can never be too careful. The first rule of write club, save your story in more than one location. And with that, I put my laptop in my case, and rush to get ready. I don't think they would appreciate the pajama pants and bedhead.

Oh, the glamorous look of an author in her element. Not. A quick shower, and a stylish updo later, I'm headed for the train. Though I'm not living in the big city, I'm close enough that a one-hour train ride will get me there. Win, win. I get to enjoy small-town life, and nature at its finest, but one hour on the train, and it's another world. I love the train. The click, click, click of the train chugging along the tracks. It's not like the subway or a bus. There is something so grand and old-world like on a real train. Not to mention, I can sit and write.

I bet the authors that wrote cowboy books would be so inspired on a train. Shoot. Distracted again. The horn from the Uber making me quite aware. Thanking the driver for waiting, we are on our way. I board the train in a nick of time, taking my seat.

I'm in my own little world right now. A brilliant plot twist has entered my mind. I just need to get it down before it's too late. "Ahem." The sound of the male voice barely registers. "Excuse me, miss." When I finish typing the sentence, my eyes raise to him slowly. *Wow. Now, this man is book worthy.* Dark hair and groomed beard. The steal your soul blue eyes that match his obviously, tailored suit. The blue and white pin striped shirt, unbuttoned with no tie. *Yes, now this fine specimen will definitely find his way into my bedroom. I mean bed. BOOK, dang it!* "Pardon me?" the man says, grumpily.

Did I say that out loud? Please, tell me I didn't. "Oh, I'm sorry." I press my laptop to my chest, and push myself back for him to squeeze by, and he does. *What I wouldn't give to squeeze that perfect bottom directly in front of me right now. Okay, get a grip, Nila.* He takes the seat closest to the window. Normally, the train ride isn't so full. Of course, this isn't the normal time I take it either. I watch him. Mystery man is working on his phone. I've done enough people watching for research to know he's not playing a game or scrolling through a social networking site. No, he's all business.

The man starts looking at me through the corner of his eye before turning his head. He starts to speak, but just smiles. You know the one. Okay, maybe you don't. It's the uncomfortable smile you give a stranger that keeps staring at you. I get that look a lot. "I'm an author," I say, and shrug like that explains everything. "Nila. Nila Thornbush." I hold out my hand to him. He doesn't take it. *Jerk. Now, you just made it to villain status. You could have been the main character.* I scrunch my nose at him and open my laptop back up. Mr. Villain goes back to doing whatever it is he's doing. After rolling his eyes at me. Probably foreclosing on an orphanage or something. *Stupid jerk.*

Furiously, I type away. At least it's making the storyline very interesting. Jerky McVillain has given me just the twist this story needs. I can't wait to kill him off later in the book.

Now, apparently, my typing away on the keys is bugging him. "Do you mind?" he asks. *Seriously? Oh, he's definitely dying in my book!*

I open my mouth to speak, but think better of it. My lips purse shut. *I will not fight on a train. I will not fight on a train.* I repeat in my mind. *I do not look good in stripes.*

"What did you say?" he asks.

"Nothing. It was nothing at all."

When I feel the train slowing and nearing the station, I get everything put away, ready to get as far away from this ass as I can. There's another Uber waiting for me there to take me downtown. I may have purposely swung my bag over my shoulder aggressively, and grin when I hear him grunt with the contract.

I exit the train with a deviant smile, strolling to the waiting car. A hand covers mine at the handle. "Excuse me. This is my ride," comes the deep voice from behind my shoulder. *Oh, hell no. Not this guy.*

"I believe you are mistaken." I hold out my phone, showing him the app. Pulling hard on the handle, I elbow him when the door flies open. My derrière is firmly planted in the seat, and I am not getting out.

"I was wondering if both of you wouldn't mind sharing the ride. You are both going downtown, and I accepted both of you. You don't mind, do you?" The driver, a sweet looking older man asks.

"Actually," I say.

"Actually, we wouldn't mind at all," answers Jerky McVillain. He then proceeds to scoot me over.

"Are you serious right now? You do know there is a whole other door on the car, right?" I growl.

"Listen. I'm sure you are in just as much of a hurry as I am. Can you just scoot over a little more, and we get on with this?"

The sound that I make cannot be explained in words. I move over against my better judgment. Before he can get too comfortable, I lay my belongings on the seat between us, refusing to budge. I glare at him, daring him to touch anything, or move any closer. He slams the door, and stays pressed against it. I'll take any small victory I can get.

My stop is first, and I do what any other normal person would do and get out on the other side. With my items in hand, I lean into the back of the car and shout, "JERK!" before slamming the door. On the sidewalk, I graze my hand down my outfit to smooth it, then look up at the massive building before me. The doorman lets the smallest of grins slip before opening the door for me.

CHAPTER TWO

I notice my agent waiting on the
elevator and stroll up beside him. The
lobby is massive, with a desert sand color
on the walls. Marble pillars with ornate
filigree at each end. It screams money and
class. "What's the meeting about?" I ask.
He gives me a wide grin, but remains
silent. It has to be on my most recent
novel. It's due to be released next month,

and they wouldn't be pressuring me for chapters on a new one just yet. I like to stay ahead of the game, and hey, if the stories are flowing, go with it.

"Now, what would be the fun in telling you now. Just wait. There is news," he says mischievously. My smile beams. I could use some awesome news after the day I've had. Butterflies are fluttering in my stomach as we ride the elevator up. Clark is all about giving me the deets. If he's this happy, this has to be something major.

As soon as the doors open, we are greeted by Grant DuBois. He's the owner of Archer Quill, the publishing house. With his hand extended for me, we shake. He leads us to the conference room. "Nila, we are so glad you could make it. When you called to reschedule, we were worried."

"I'm so sorry. The words were flowing, and you know how that is. I didn't want to break the momentum," I play off.

"Fantastic! I'd love to hear what you have so far. Can we get you anything? Coffee, water, champagne? Ellen, can you bring in the glasses?" *Champagne?* They've never offered me that before. Eek! I sit down at the table. I'm on the edge of the seat. My foot bounces uncontrollably in anticipation. Clark places a hand on my knee to try and calm me. Grant pours, then hands Clark and I each a glass of the bubbly. I wait to take a sip until we all have one, and he makes his announcement.

"Nila. We've been monitoring the pre-orders and they are through the roof. I've passed along some early releases, and we've even been contacted by a couple of celebrities. They love what you've done and want interviews, asap. They've chosen your book to be their next big book club read. Both of them. Do you know what this means?"

I knew exactly what this meant. I am finally going to have the "best-selling author" title. They don't have to tell me which celebrities. We all know which two have the most sought-after book clubs. This is big. HUGE! Before he can say cheers, I'm downing the glass. Not only will this set me up, but it will also help past book sales. It's all a dream right now.

"We want to take you out for dinner to celebrate. Then you need to make a quick trip home to pack. You and Clark have a plane to catch late tonight. The show will pick you up when you land in Chicago, and they'll give you their itinerary from there," declares Grant. Between the news I've just received, not to mention, the second glass of champagne, my mind is spinning.

"You're very quiet, Nila. Say something."

"Are you sure you have the right author? I mean, they really want ME in Chicago? Tonight?" I ask. Grant, Clark, and some of the others that surround me in the office chuckle and smile.

"Yes, you, Nila Thornbush. You are going to be the next New York Times Best Selling Author. Of course, there are a few other titles you are going to be holding soon." Grant holds his hand out for me to stand. "You have a couple hours before our reservations. We have a car waiting downstairs if you would like to do some shopping for the interview. There won't be time after you get to Chicago."

"That would be lovely," I say. Okay, so that's something that would not normally come out of my mouth, but I feel the need to be more proper than, "Hell, to the yeah!"

I feel like Vivian on Rodeo Drive with Edward's giant stack of cash. The only difference is, I'm not dressed like a prostitute, and it's my own card. Not unlimited, but there is definitely enough on there to get a few nicer outfits for the trip. The dress pants and blouse from the local shopping mall that I'm wearing aren't going to cut it.

That makes me think of tailored suit guy. I scrunch my nose in disgust. Why did he pop into my head? Ah, yeah, the clothes that were made just for him. That's the look I want. Not a suit for a man, mind you. However, something so amazing that it looks like it is made for me, and me only. We are let out at the nicest boutique in the city. Clark opens the door and lets me in first. That's when I spot it across the room.

The dress. When I try it on the fabric is so luxurious. I stand in front of the mirrors. It accentuates all the curves, in all the right ways. The color compliments my complexion and makes my eyes pop. This is the one.

Clark lets out a soft whistle, and I can see his reflection behind me. I'm not sure which of us is beaming with more pride. Me, or him. He's been by my side ever since I took the leap from indie to traditionally published. Don't get me wrong, I loved being an indie author. Every single bit of the book is mine. Well, except for editing and cover design. That, I was smart enough to leave for the professionals. The marketing, formatting, and everything else is all me. It was so much work. That definitely cut into my writing time. I eventually made decent money. Nothing compared to when I was picked up by Archer Quill, but it was good. Now the percentages I get are smaller, but the exposure, and increase in my name getting out there is huge. That, in turn, increased my bank account.

Dinner is amazing. Never have I been to a place so fancy. My hair and dress make me feel glamorous. I say something that strikes the rest of my table funny. That causes me to throw my head back and laugh hysterically with them. When I lower my head, that's when I notice him. The man from the train is here, in my restaurant. Okay, so, it isn't my restaurant, but it is my big night. Why, of all the places, is he here? Seeing the man from the train is a surprise. What is surprising me more, though, is that strange look he is giving me. Granted, I hadn't dated in such a long time, but I swear that its lust in his eyes. For me? I can't think about this now. This is my night, and I'm enjoying it.

Why do I keep feeling his eyes on me? Maybe, because, I steal glances, too? It doesn't stop me from licking the chocolate off my fork. Or maybe, subconsciously, that's why I am. Grant paid the check for the table. Clark and I thank him and say goodbye, and he escorts me outside. I am still on cloud nine as I step out into the warm evening air.

CHAPTER THREE

This morning couldn't have gotten any worse. My car broke down, and my normal commute into the city is not possible. I pop the hood, trying to assess what's wrong. Let's be honest, I have no clue what I'm doing, and there is no way I'm ruining my one good suit. My father always told me that with one really good suit, you can take over the world. I didn't want the world. Just my little corner of it. The suit had cost me several months' salary. It's worth it, though, tailored just for me. It made me feel like I could do anything in it. I slam the hood and pull out my phone.

I could have Ben come pick me up. That would make us both late. This meeting is too important to miss. My clients who had flown in were not going to allow a merger with a someone that couldn't even manage to be on time. Ben had to be there in the unforeseen event that I couldn't. He is my partner. We built this company together from a late-night dorm room vision, to what it is now. I wouldn't let him down.

There's only one seat available, and I have to get it next to some oblivious twit who is just staring at me, mute. I finally get her to let me squeeze past her. *Oh great, now she wants to be chatty.* I blow her off, continuing to get my small staff prepared for the meeting. This has to go off without a hitch. If we can get the backing needed, our company will finally take off. Instead of a staff of five, who knows how many jobs this could create. This site has endless possibilities.

I swear that woman just muttered something about not looking good in stripes. Is she talking about her, or me? She's not dressed like a psychopath. Not that I would know how one dressed. I know she can't be talking about my shirt.

The Uber will be waiting for me as soon as I get off the train. When the train pulls to a stop, I stand, impatiently waiting for the woman next to me to exit. Leaping off the last step, I rush for the Uber. My mind is on the meeting. Absentminded, I stop at my transportation. I reach for the handle of the door at the same time as someone else. My hand touching that of someone much softer. Of course, it's the woman that had hit me with her bag on the way out. How can someone be so rude? I quickly try to explain that it's my Uber. However, she demands that it's hers. This crazy person shoves her phone in my face as some sort of proof. I'm about to pull my own phone out, when the driver leans his head out the window.

The driver "suggests" that we both take it into the city. At this point, I don't care. I need to get going. Trying to scoot her over a little so I can get in, is a feat in itself. Why couldn't she just scoot over already? The other side of the car is blocked by another vehicle trying to pull out. I'm not taking the chance of getting crushed between the two. She's ranting something about going to the other side, but I'm not giving her the satisfaction of engagement.

I squeeze in, shut the door and we are now, silently, on our way.

We arrive to her stop first. A tall gray brick building, with a onyx and gold sign reading Archer Quill Publishing. I guess she wasn't lying about being an author. Or maybe she's just a want to be author. Who knows? *Great, now she's rambling again and calling me a jerk.* I ignore her because I refuse to lower myself to her level. A few blocks later, I'm hopping out, dashing upstairs to my office, my briefcase in one hand. My fingers crossed with the other.

I look up to the sky before entering, and give my dad a silent plea to be with me as I make this important proposal. What I wouldn't give for him to still be here. Making him proud is what I've always tried to do in my life. Even after his was taken from him too soon.

As soon as the elevator door opens, Ben's there waiting on me. "What the hell, Blake? You know how important this is." I roll my eyes at him. Its either that or punch him.

"Like I had any control over my car biting the dust. Are they here yet?" I ask.

"Not yet. The conference room is all set up. Have you got everything?" Ben asks. I pat my briefcase and head towards the conference room. I run my hands across the leather before opening it. It was my father's. He gave it to me the first day we started this company. The gold emblem with Chandler engraved on it brushes across my fingers. Not as new and shiny as it had been as a child, but it warmed my heart just the same.

I click open the locks and pull out my laptop and folders, laying them on the table. Linking into the screen on the wall, I set up the video presentation. The folders are laid in front of each chair neatly. I take a deep breath. This is it. The elevator dings, and Ben and I make our way to welcome our guests.

"Mr. Hanover, Mr. Benson, I'm so glad you could make it," I greet with my hand outstretched.

"Your determination for this meeting, I didn't think we had a choice," answers Mr. Hanover. I try not to clench my jaw, but fail.

"Now Bob. You and I both know we wouldn't be here if we weren't intrigued," replies Mr. Benson, patting his partner's shoulder as they entered the room. Now this guy, I can work with. It eases some tension that I didn't know I had been holding in.

They take a seat as my assistant, Susan, pours them some ice water from the pitcher. She then offers them some pastries that were displayed on the table. These weren't your typical bagels and donuts. We got the most delicious baked goods from a little shop a few blocks away, Scents and Bake Ability. One bite of anything they made, and you were hooked. It is all that good. Proof is seeing old Bob's face light up after a taste. Ben gives me a look. I give him the slightest grin in return.

I open up the folder, and start the presentation. The video is not just showing them the boring statistics, but our vision. They seem genuinely impressed. I can tell Ben is holding his breath. By the time I show them the last slide, I too, am lacking a breath or two.

"Would you mind giving us a moment?" asks Mr. Benson. We nod and exit the room.

Across the office space, we step into my office and shut the glass door, watching the two discuss what they had seen. "How do you think it went?" I ask Ben.

"They'd be crazy not to take this offer. Right?" he questions nervously, wringing his hands together, looking towards the other room. The other pair didn't talk long before Mr. Benson is giving Bob another pat on the shoulder. Both turned in their seats and motioned for us to return.

We reentered the conference room, taking the seats opposite them. A piece of paper slid across the table to us. "You have some really impressive ideas about where you want to take this. We'd like to be a part of it, and this is what we can offer you." Slowly, my hand reaches out for the paper. I look to my partner before opening. I let out a breath, and unfold the paper. I look to Ben who is trying not to give away a look of shock. Looking down at the paper again, I try to stay calm and fold it back. "Do we have a deal, young men?"

I'm the first one out of my seat and stretching my hand across the table. "We most certainly have a deal. We look forward to being in business with you. The papers can be drawn up by the end of the day."

"We actually have our own with us. If you would like to have your lawyer go over them, we are staying at the Majestic. Our flight leaves at ten tomorrow morning." Mr. Hanover pops his own briefcase, handing over the contract before rising. We shake hands before they leave, agreeing to meet for dinner later to sign the papers. Right before the elevator closes, he calls out,

"Those honey, almond, beehive things. Where do I get more of them?"

"Take a right when you exit the building. It's three blocks away. I'll tell Carmella you are on your way," I say with a chuckle. As soon as the door closes, we both jump in the air and high-five. Ben let's out some whoops. I grab Susan, giving her a spin, and dance her across the room.

My middle-aged assistant laughs and squeezes my face. "I knew you boys could do it! I'm so proud of you. Your father is looking down on you and smiling, Blake." I take her hand, and kiss her palm, then cup it to my cheek. After my father's death, I had her come work for us. She kept my father's business running. There is no way I am going to let that one go. Susan is an asset to our small company.

CHAPTER FOUR

Our lawyer, well, actually, my friend Alex, goes over all the fine print. He assures us it's legit. Ben and I ride over to the restaurant we are meeting them at. We take a spot at the bar until our party arrives. Taking a sip of the amber liquid, my pal nods to the table behind us which can only mean one thing, a beautiful woman. A party of five laughs at something the woman said. Her head is thrown back in carefree bliss. She's stunning. There is something about an attractive woman and a real, not held back, laugh.

The joyous look suddenly stops when her gaze locks with mine. Her. I recognize that glare. It's the woman from the train and cab ride. The man next to her says something and she gives a smile, but that one doesn't reach her eyes as the one before. Pity. She was so much more attractive just moments ago. I turn back to the bar and order another drink.

"Wow. What did you do to her?" Ben asks when he notices the vibe in the room change. "Jilted lover?"

"Hardly. Some lunatic I met on the train earlier," I say and take a big drink.

"That lunatic is smokin'. Did you see who she's with? That's the big wig over at Archer Quill Publishing. She must be an author they're wooing," Ben says.

"She mentioned something about writing, or being an author, or something. I don't really remember," I say casually.

"You don't remember? I know this deal is important, but when a beautiful woman like that talks to you, you pay attention."

"She's alright," I say. I'm lying through my teeth. She exudes beauty. Her hair, no longer in the tight updo from earlier. Now, it seems softer. Two loose tendrils fall to the sides. I imagine my hands fisting the silkiness, as I take her into a deep kiss. Her clothing is different, as well. Her curves more sensuous. My slacks get tight as I picture her pressed against my body. *Reel it in, Blake. You can't be signing contracts with a raging hard on.*

I look towards the door and notice the other two have arrived. The hostess leads them to us, and the four of us follow her to our table. One more look in her direction before we are seated. The disdain on her face changes when she sees the difference in mine. The look that I'm giving her is pure heat. Hers is that of confusion. Not knowing whether to be angry or intrigued.

Dinner is pleasant. We sign the contract, and get to know our new business partners. Even though it seems like both tables have something to celebrate, theirs is definitely more relaxed. While we discuss the plans for the future, they laugh and joke. I find my eyes being drawn to her throughout the meal.

After ours is over, we shake and walk outside. Ben offers to give me a ride home, but I decline. My gut tells me to take the last train out of town tonight. Just as my ride arrives, I open the door and look to the restaurant. She steps out, brighter than every star in the sky. The mystery woman stops in her tracks when she sees mc holding the door... for her. I mouth the words, "truce?" She leans over and kisses one of the men on the cheek before walking my way. Without a word, the woman climbs elegantly into the vehicle. I shut the door, and walk to the other side and get in.

We ride in awkward silence to the station. She fumbles through her purse before speaking. "If it's not too much trouble, could we pick up my laptop and packages?"

"No problem, miss," says the driver. She gives him the directions. This time, her items stay on her lap instead of between us. *Well, there's progress.*

I break the silence and hold out my hand. "Blake. Blake Chandler. I need to apologize for this morning. My car broke down, and I had this important meeting."

"It's fine. I was kind of having my own day," she says softly.

"It's not fine. I was rude. I shouldn't have taken it out on you."

"You're right," she says. I look at her, anger crawling up my skin, until I see her face. She sheepishly smiles and shrugs. It's one of those smiles, you can't help to give back. "So, everything worked out, okay?" she asks.

Nodding, I answer, "Yes, better than I could have hoped for, actually. What about you? It looked like you were celebrating, yourself?"

"Better than my best dream." She relaxes back into the seat with the brightest, most genuine smile, and a sigh.

"I'm glad." Before I can ask her what her best dream consisted of, we are pulling up to the station. I jump out first, so I can open her door. Holding my elbow out for her to take, I say, "your chariot awaits, fair Nila." Surprised that I remembered her name, her lips turn up and she places her hand on my arm.

We sit together, by choice this time. I ask her about herself. She tells me all about her latest book, her flight tonight, and interview tomorrow. I make a mental note to start to DVR that celebrity, so I don't miss it.

Nila asks about my meeting. She congratulates me on the merger. As she got lost in telling me about her writing, I get lost in my business. I tell her how Ben and I came up with the idea for our software program, and its capabilities to change the face of marketing. We have come up with a plan to link small businesses and sole proprietors into one online location, one search engine. Then, allow them to connect with people all over the world. I know there are other programs that are similar, but ours will be legitimate, qualified people. Not just anyone with a log-in can sign up and try to sell their products or talents. Unlike Sixxett, where the purchaser has their fingers crossed whether or not it's a scam.

I blush and stop. "Sorry, I'm rambling."

"No, it's fascinating. I wish there was something like that when I was indie. Finding the right people isn't always easy." I give her a questioning look. She continues. "Before I became traditionally published, I was an indie author." Another blank look from me. She chuckles. "Independent author. I did all the work from finding someone to edit, to cover art, and before I learned myself, how to format a book for paperback or Ebook sales. Then there's finding a good PA when things got a little busier. It was hard finding someone you could trust to give you what you needed with what little revenue you had. If it wasn't for Clark, I don't know what I'd have done."

Jealousy crept up me at the mention of another man. As she went on, I realized he is nothing more than an agent and friend. Watching her soft, full lips as she spoke, my mind went directly to wanting to give her what she needed. I can't help myself. I am a man after all. The train ride is entirely too short, and I want to continue the evening. That is going to be impossible with her having to rush home to pack. As I watched her speed away in her Uber, I realized I didn't even get her number. *Idiot!*

CHAPTER FIVE

I turn to look behind me, and give a wave to the handsome man from the train. Now facing forward, I replay the day in my head. It's funny how things work out. Two people, both having bad days, taking it out on the other. Push away all the stress of the day, and there's a connection. How many other people in this big, 'ol world are missing their own connections by letting the mishaps of life get to them? People, day after day, pushing away "the one," and not even knowing it because they let whatever it is, manipulate how people see them. It's crazy to think about.

The ride home has me imagining how he tastes. How would he be at kissing? Would it be soft and sweet, or urgent and full of need? I'm guessing the latter with the look he was giving me back at the restaurant. That man oozed sex. That thought is going to have to wait until another time. Like when I finally made it to the hotel, hours from now.

As soon as I got home, I made a quick pot of coffee. The boost of caffeine is exactly what I need to get everything done at lightning speed. Clark is packing for himself, then coming to come pick me up in his car. We had three hours to make it to the airport to catch our flight. This is so exciting! With so much to do, Blake hadn't even crossed my mind again until we boarded, and the plane took off.

"So, who was the stranger at the restaurant you left with?" Clark asked with a wink. As we lift off into the sky, I fill him in on the day. How we both hated the other. Then, after dinner, how amazing the train ride with Blake was. "Wow! Sounds like there's a to be continued. Are you going to call him after the taping?"

"Oh, my God! Clark! I didn't get his number. I was in such a hurry to get home and pack; I didn't ask for it. Are you freaking kidding me?" I slump in the seat, defeated. "Do you know how long it's been since a guy even piqued my interest?"

"Three years," he answers.

"Huh?" I ask.

"Three years, four months and let me see... twelve days to be exact." I give him a questioning look. "Babe, that's how long it's been since I came into your chaotic life." He elbows me gently in the side.

"Yes," I say. Then I elbow him back. "Too bad you weren't won over by my feminine charms."

"Hey. You charmed me into being your agent. Lucky for your roommate Rick, I only had eyes for him."

"You still owe me a roommate, you thief. One that can cook as phenomenal as him. Of course, my clothes say otherwise. I actually lost fifteen pounds after he moved out."

"Yeah, you wench. I found it." God, I love this guy. Not only has he sling-shotted me into success, but he's also became my best friend. Besides Rick, of course. They are the perfect couple. If I could hand pick anyone in the whole world for Rick, it was Clark.

"So, what am I going to do about Blake? I don't know where he lives, works, or his number. I'm never going to see him again, am I? I'm destined to be a spinster."

"Dramatic much? Seriously, Nila. If it's meant to be, you will see him again. Besides, you have a lot on your plate right now. You've got not one, but two big, televised interviews, a new book to write, signings, and so much more. You, yourself, said he was an ass."

"He apologized. Plus, we had a great time on the last train home. Did you see how that man looked? Did you?"

"Yes, he is extremely fine. There is more to life than looks." That's when I give him a look. Of course, I know that looks aren't everything. It's just that I haven't dated in a long time and well, come on, looks don't hurt. Clark's right, though. If it's meant to be, we'll reconnect. That's how all the best stories end.

I try to doze off, but the coffee from earlier has me wired. Let's hope their makeup artist can conceal these bags I'm bound to be rocking by the interview. I'm at that state of exhaustion where nothing makes sense. I can't think straight. Dear Lord, please don't let me get to the point where everything is hilarious, and I can't stop laughing. It's not pretty.

I did a rock-a-thon once. By hour twenty-four, something struck me funny. I laughed and cried for over an hour without being able to stop. I mean, it was cool at the time. We were teenagers and the other "rockers" had the same effect. Seven teens uncontrollably laughing and rocking the night away. It was rocking chairs, by the way. I don't think we would have made it if we were dancing or musically rocking that long. We did make a lot of money for our fundraiser. Not as much as when we made peanut rolls, but we all got to go to the youth convention.

Maybe if I daydream. That sometimes works to knock me out. I close my eyes, and replay the train ride. The enjoyable one. Then I take it forward. In my mind, I picture me about to walk away. My heart says don't leave. I turn to look back, and he's chasing the car. The driver stops. I jump out, running to him. It's dark and raining. Our arms outstretched like some cheesy movie. I am wrapped into his arms directly under a golden streetlight glow. He kisses and spins me. All is right with the world. His fingers are lost in my beautifully, perfect locks. Which is a little confusing, considering it's raining. That's when he draws me in even closer. His muscles are surrounding me. Blake pulls back, and stares into my eyes. He speaks. "The plane will be landing soon. Please adjust your seats into the upright position, and fasten your safety belts."

"Huh?" I look at him confused. Then, I awaken by Clark nudging me. Dang it. I'm on a plane.

CHAPTER SIX

We get to the fancy hotel they set us up in. I sink into the luxurious bed. The comforter, like a warm hug from a feathered angel. The pillows are equally divine. Twisting, I cocoon myself in. The last thing I think of before letting sleep take me over is, *wouldn't it be wonderful to stay in this bed forever?*

LAST TRAIN

The phone on my nightstand sings to me. *Hozier* serenading me with *Movement* stirs me from my slumber. I can't remember sleeping this great. I'm half expecting the bedroom to be surrounded by woodland creatures greeting me for the day. Pressing snooze, I sink back in, knowing that the next time his voice fills my ears, I need to rise. And I do. Gathering up my travel bag, I make my way to the bathroom. This is not your typical hotel decor. It has a tub, a big one, and it's calling my name. Surely, there's enough time for a bubble bath. The steaming water fills, and I decide another cup of java is just what I need. I pop in one of the pods, the aroma of coffee wafting through the air. Adding the perfect blend of sugar and creamer, I take the first sip. Clarity, awakening, and motivation course through my veins, and fills me as the cup empties. A thought pops in my head that maybe I need help for my caffeine addiction. Then, I decide that if I have to have an addiction, this ones pretty tame.

Promising myself I won't lose track of time in the tub, I set another alarm. It's a good thing I did. I definitely would still be in it. Toweling the bubbles from my legs, I dry myself. Not sure if they style my hair or not, I grab the dryer and my hair products.

A knock sounds at the door. Tightening the towel around me, I crack it to find Clark. He pushes his way in. His own special way of telling me to hurry up. I make quick work of my hair, and grab my new outfit. "Do they do my makeup, or do I?"

"How do I know?" he asks.

"You're supposed to be the guy with all the answers," I reply.

"Just bring it with you just in case."

"Good idea. Well, I guess I'm ready if you are." At that moment, the phone rings to let us know there is a car downstairs waiting for us. "Perfect timing."

The rest of the day is rush, and wait, rush, and wait. My head is spinning. Everything is a blur. After it's over, I honestly can't tell you one thing I said, or if it was any good. Well, it's done and over now. Clark has his hands clasped and he's beaming back at me. That's definitely a good sign. "Did I do, okay? I was so nervous. Tell me I didn't mess up."

"You, my darling, are made for the spotlight," Clark says, taking my hand and spinning me.

The star of the show walks over, shaking my hand. "Great interview. It's a pleasure meeting you. Congratulations on your new book. It's going to really soar."

"Thank you. That means a lot coming from you," I say, fangirling. As she walks away, I turn to Clark, "EEK!" My feet doing a happy dance in my heels, while holding Clark's hands.

In the towncar, Clark is texting with Grant and checking the numbers on his phone. His mouth drops open. "You are not going to believe the pre-order numbers!" Turning it so I can see the message, it's now me gaping. *This can't be real!* We stop at a high-end boutique, before checking out, and catching a flight for the next interview. *Is this really my life?*

With this interview, I'm not quite so nervous. I actually remember parts of it. She's so sweet and down-to-earth. It's more like two girlfriends catching up.

Again, the numbers skyrocket. Mentally calculating, I'm going to surpass my advance they gave me, probably on the day it releases! The royalties, even with them taking a good chunk, will set me up for years to come.

My heart sinks. Clark sees something in my face that has him concerned. When he asks me what's wrong, it all spills out.

"I can afford a new car. A nice one even."

"And that's a problem, why?"

"If I get a new car, I can go anywhere. If I can go anywhere, I don't need the train. I don't take the train; I don't see Blake. We don't reconnect, fall in love, make babies. I'll die a rich, lonely woman with a house full of cats," I ramble.

"Oh, good grief, Nila. Drama much. You are the only, and I mean only, person who can take something fabulous, twist, and warp it. Stop over-thinking. Bask. Enjoy."

"You're right. I'm being irrational. I'm going to be rich. We're going to be rich."

"Damn right, we." He pats my knee, I calm down. Most writers must have a mind that races, goes overboard, and beyond. That's where all the stories begin. For me, writing has been a way of quieting that mash-up of thoughts. It gives me cerebral peace. I haven't been able to write for days now. That's all it is. Let me get back to me and my stories, everything will be fine.

Clark offers to give me a ride home once we are off the plane. I ask that he drops me off at the train station. He rolls his eyes, but obliges. The ride is quiet. Just the sound on the tracks. The whisper of hushed conversations. No snarky man next to me. No rendezvous and deep talks. The train chugging along to take me to my lonely home.

This is ridiculous. I should be on cloud nine right now. *Shake off this melancholy, Nila. You miss a hot guy on a train, boo hoo. Remember, he was an ass hat the first ride.* My mind wanders. *Oh, but that second one.* Laptop, that's what I need. Pulling the flat computer out of the case, my hand brushes across it. I walk to my desk, plug it in and open. My screen beckons me, the cover of my first book. Double click, now I see the last chapter I had been working on. Chuckling, I realize how mad I was when I wrote this. I start to delete it. Highlight, cut... dang it, paste. It's really too good to throw away.

Pantser that I am, the story unfolds as I type away. It takes on its own life, and I have no control. My fingers eventually cramp. Popping, cracking them, I look up to see the sun start to rise out the window.

Did I really spend the whole night writing?

Clicking on the project targets icon, I gasp.

Twelve thousand words without stopping.

That might be a record. My arms above

me, I stretch. I need sustenance, and

make my way to the pantry. I grab a box

of snack cakes, and return to my desk.

Just a few more sentences, I tell myself.

Famous last words.

CHAPTER SEVEN

BLAKE

Every morning, I get up and ready for work. Day after day, I trudge to my now fixed car, knowing I have zero chance of seeing Nila this way. Every morning, every evening, I pass the station, hoping to catch a glimpse of her waiting. It's been two months now. Why didn't I get her number? *Such an idiot!*

Ben wads a paper, tossing it at my head. "Get your head in the game, Blake. Please do not tell me your still thinking about the girl at the restaurant. You are, aren't you?" All I can do is shrug. No sense in denying it. "Have you done the last run on the software? Is it ready? We've only got a few more weeks to check out the lists of people, and get them set up. The last thing we need is to end up like our competitors. The whole point of this is to make sure we have legitimate, independent, professionals that can provide quality services. Our whole brand is to be known as a site you can trust."

"I know this. The software is good to go, no glitches so far. I have ten people lined up today to meet in person and check out their portfolios. Then, another twenty tomorrow by video. Trust me, I'm still handling business. What about you?" That sounded way too snarky. I can see by Ben's face; I went a little too far. Ben stomps out.

A normal apology isn't going to cut it. He's not just a coworker, he's my best friend. Ben's right, I need to get this girl outta my head. Knock. Knock. My knuckles tap lightly on his glass door. "Listen. I'm sorry. You're absolutely right. I've gotta get her outta my head. If you're still down for O'Malley's after work, we'll go."

Ben's devious smile lets me know we're still good. "Finally! It's about time. Now, give me some of the folders. I'll help you weed through some possible people. How do you have them organized?"

I run to my office and grab a huge stack of files, dropping them with a thud onto Ben's desk. "These are just musicians. I have them by occupation. Singers, editing services, voice actors... don't get me started on cover designers. Artists who draw covers, others who use photo layers, vectors. I am over my head right now. Your article is a hit. There are hundreds and hundreds of people wanting to be on this app. It's just a matter of checking out their qualifications, fees, reviews from other sites. I know there are easier ways, but I want to know 100% that no one on our site is going to feel scammed."

"I'm right there with you, partner. I have all the marketing set up to go live on the first. The reach on all the promotions is going to be out of this world. Advertising is all ready. I'll help you narrow down the candidates this week. If you want, I'll start setting up all the profiles next week, while you finish checking the others out. That work?"

"That would be great. I thought about promoting Susan. Letting her take some of this on, as well. I mean, we're going to hire more staff anyway. What do you think of that?" I ask.

"Yeah, definitely. Can we put her in charge of finding us assistants as perfect as her?"

"Well, of course. We'd be crap at choosing her replacement. No one can be a Susan. Do we tell her now?"

"She deserves a cake or something, right? Let me call the bakery, see what they have." Ben whips out his pocket phone, calling the shop. He gives me a thumbs up, telling them to save it, we'll pick it up in a few minutes.

I volunteered to go. The fresh air will do me good. The season is changing. It's still on the warmer side of autumn, but a crispness is edging its way in. You can feel it coming. The leaves are beginning their evolution of green, to all the amazing colors of fall. It's probably my favorite time of year. Cool enough you can wear your suit and not sweat, but not so cool you need a coat yet. I wish it could be like this day all year round. The slight breeze lightens my mood. The sounds of the city around me. People shuffling to and fro, passing by each other. A newsstand selling the latest magazines and daily papers. Strangers looking their best in their business attire. One of them catches my eye, as I cross the busy street at the light. I pause to take another look. Could it be her? A long-haired beauty looking up, shielding her eyes from the midday sun.

I call out her name, "NILA!" The sound of my voice, lost in the crowd. Making a mad dash across the intersection, I hold out my hand to the cars coming my way. A cab honks at me, with the driver yelling at me. It doesn't discourage me. I run for it.

For her. "NILA!" My hand waving furiously to get her to take notice. The woman stops in her tracks and turns, looking this way and that. She spots me, finally. Her eyelids snap wide in surprise. It's the curve of her lips into a smile, that gets me. Makes almost getting flattened by a delivery van worth it.

Nila gives me a huge wave, and a signal to stay put. She dashes to me. The clicking of her heels on the pavement in such a pace is impressive. How do women do it every day? When she reaches me, we are wrapped in an embrace. Just like long-lost friends, finally reunited. Nila's feet lift off the ground, as I hug her. Probably too intimate for someone I had only met not even a handful of times. There's something that warms my heart as she hugs me back. As I gently set her back down, she pulls away from me to give me a good look. Still holding my hands out in front. "I can't believe it's you! It's been so long."

"I see that your writing career has taken off. What are you doing here with the commoners?" I tease.

This causes the cutest pink flush to her cheeks. Her head dips, and I tuck the stray strand of hair behind her ear. "I'm not that famous. What about you, Mr. Entrepreneur? Aren't you busy taking the Internet by storm?"

It's me that is embarrassed this time. I kick the toe of my dress shoe against the pavement. "Well, I'm trying, anyway. Where are you headed off to?"

"I'm trying to find this bakery everyone keeps raving about. Apparently, I've taken a wrong turn, or two. It's called Scents and Bake Ability. Do you know it?" she asks.

"You have definitely taken a wrong turn, my dear. I am actually heading there now." She quirks an unbelieving eyebrow at me. "Really! I am on my way to get a surprise cake for our assistant we are promoting. Well, as soon as, I get back with it."

She slides her arm into mine, "By all means, lead the way, handsome." We walk, arm in arm, casually down the other way. I cracked a joke about the cabby yelling, and almost dying to see her. The way she put her hand over mine, throwing her head carelessly back and laughing, did something to me just then. This time, oh yes, this time; I wasn't going to let her get away.

CHAPTER EIGHT

BLAKE

We entered the little bakery, with a ting sounding above the door. Nila closed her eyes, and took in the sweet smells of it. The way she never takes anything for granted, charms me. Nila is the kind of women that takes pleasure in all that surrounds her. Even I had to close my eyes, just so I could experience this moment like her. Scents of fresh bread,

honey, vanilla, cinnamon filled my head.
Glazed pastries, cookies, and cakes take
over my senses.

"Welcome! Oh, Blake. It's you. Who's
your pretty friend?" Carmella asks, her
smile friendly and bright.

"See, I told you I was coming here. I'm
one of Carmella's best customers.
Carmella, meet the talented author, Nila
Thornbush."

"Shut up! Are you kidding me? You're
thee Nila Thornbush? The one that wrote,
My Day in the Sun? *That* Nila? Oh my God!
I've read all your books!" Carmella is
seriously fan-girling now. Is she really that
famous, and I never knew? I guess I need
to check out her books. Nila is shy, but
friendly. Me, however, am bursting with
pride for her. Not to mention, her hand has
slid down and is now clasped with mine.

"That's me. Now you. You, my dear, are the best-known bake shop in town. From what I've seen and smelled, I see why. Now, I have no idea what to pick. It all looks so decadent. How about you just give me a box. A big one, with a little of everything."

"I will hook you up. On one condition. You sign my book. I have it in the back," Carmella answers.

"Sounds like a good deal to me. Blake here, I believe he is here to pick up a cake." I nod.

"It's about time you gave Susan a big promotion. She's been keeping you and Ben in line for years," the baker says with a twinkle in her eye. She turns and walks to the back, coming back with both a cake in its box, and her hard-cover book. She sets them on the counter, and before Nila can snatch it, I grab the book. The cover is stunning, very ornate. I peak under the paper cover, noticing the book itself also embellished. Embossed in gold, my fingers trail over her name, Nila Thornbush. With both hands, I flip through the pages, noticing the ones with each chapter heading, have a sunflower that fill the page. Ever so light, under the printed words. A lot of thought was put into the creation of this book.

"Did your publisher design all this?" I say. My head slightly tilted looking down at her.

"No. This one is all me, back when I was an indie, just starting out. I mean, I didn't do the sunflower, or the cover. I had them out-sourced. That is above my level of expertise. I had a vision, then found someone who could make it happen."

"You know. I could really use your help. Your knowledge on this is exactly what I need. What are you doing today?" I ask.

She gives me a shrug. "Nothing now. This was my last stop before going to the train station." She gave me a look that told me she said something she shouldn't.

"You're still taking the train?" I ask.

"I mean... there was a certain someone I met once on a train. A girl could hope, right?" The flush again crossing her cheeks. My stomach does a flip. Could Nila be feeling the same? She looked up to me. "What do you need help with?"

"I could really use some input from an author's perspective on some clients on the app we're working on. Someone from the front lines, so to speak. Can I steal you away? There's cake in it for ya," I say, and give her a wink.

"Well, why didn't you say that to start with. Count me in. You'll have to give me a ride home, though," Nila mentioned, then bit her bottom lip.

"Miss Thornbush, I would love to give you a ride home."

"When the two of you are done flirting. I have her box ready. Of course, I am rather enjoying seeing this side of you, Blake. Forget what I said. Flirt away," says Carmella, the store owner. She's right. It's rare that I'm ever this, I don't know, carefree? This woman definitely brings it out in me. I pull out my wallet, paying for everything, though Nila protested. She finally relented, and only signed the book.

I carefully carry the two boxes, as we stroll back to my building. My phone starts buzzing. With my hands full, I ask her to grab it out of my pocket. When she showed me the screen with Ben's name across the front, I knew I was in trouble for taking so long. That's why I let her answer.

"Hello," she said in a sing-song voice. I tried to hold back my laughter, because I knew without a doubt, Ben had an angry lecture on the tip of his tongue. My mind pictures his mouth gaping open, then looking down to see if he dialed the right number. I know my friend.

"No, you have the right number. Blake has his hands full at the moment." Nailed it. "No, he doesn't have his hands full of me. He's holding Susan's cake if you must know." That asshole better not be talking to her like I think he is. "Me. I'm Nila. We are heading to the office right now." I'm not sure what he just said to her, but now she's giggling. "Oh, he has, has he?" Her kitten-lapping-cream smile she gave me has me dying to know. We're at the front of the building. I fumble at the door handle. She holds a finger to me, to wait just a second. "Well, Benny. We've made it here. I'll definitely keep that in mind. Talk soon." Nila ends the call and swings open the door holding it for me. Benny? She called him Benny.

As we stood on the elevator, I finally ask. "So, what did old Benny have to say?" Seriously, I needed to know.

"You guys are really close. Aren't you?" she asks.

"Yeah. And you're changing the subject. What'd he say?" I plead.

"Oh, look. Here's your floor," she pushed her way out to avoid answering.

CHAPTER NINE

The impromptu, promotion celebration I invaded is sweet. Susan is so surprised and honored. "Who would have thought, at sixty, I would have such a title. Are you sure, this is what you want to do?"

"Of course," they say in unison.

"You know this business as well as Ben and me, maybe better. Of course, you'll

have to find your replacement. Plus, hire
an assistant for yourself," says Blake.

"Me? I get an assistant, too?"

"Well, yeah," says Ben.

"I know just the person. I'll give her a
call. But first, let's dive into this cake." She
does the honor of cutting it, and I place
the pieces on paper plates. As we nosh on
this moist and sweet concoction, we chat. I
can tell she loves both of them dearly. It's
not just a work bond they share. Susan
starts fulfilling her new duties, while Blake
and I go over candidates for the website in
his office.

I am leaning over Blake. We are going
over who we think would be a great fit,
and those that are just posers. We are so
close. My hair tickles his cheek. His scent,
being this close, is stirring things inside me
that have been hibernating for oh, so long.
His cologne, a mix of amber, spice, and

walking in the woods with autumn leaves stirring. My nose wants to burrow into his neck, taking it in. I want to kiss him, working my way around to his lips. Closer and closer, I lean into him. So intoxicating. My fingers brush my hair back over my shoulder, barely touching his skin. Blake inhales sharply. Can I be affecting him just as much? Let's see.

"This one right here," I point to the computer screen, "just copies other artists."

His face turns to me. "How do you know? How do you know this person isn't original?" My gaze turns to him. Blake's eyes aren't looking into mine. He's staring at my lips. I bite my lower one, looking just as intently. *Kiss me, kiss me now. Please.* The phone rings, breaking the moment. Standing straighter, stepping back, I remove myself from his personal space. That was close. It is all I could do not to make the first move.

"Would you excuse me? It seems, Susan has already interviewed someone and wants our final approval. It shouldn't take long."

"No, go right ahead. I can flip through some of these, and make some notes if you want."

"That would be fantastic! Thanks for all the help you've given me today. I'll be right back." I nod at him, taking his now empty seat in front of the computer. This really is going to be a great way for people to connect with the talent they need from anywhere in the world. The fact that they are taking this so seriously, only confirms the success they are going to have. The other site is so sketchy. You really don't know if you are going to get the quality and originality that you're paying for. I take notes, jotting down whether or not I believe them to be good choices. Blake had come back in, and I hadn't even heard the door.

"You've been busy," he says. The tenor of his voice, pleasantly causing tingles along my skin.

"Just jotting some things down for you."

"Would you go out with me?" My head whips around to look into his smoky eyes. He's serious. "I want to take you to dinner."

"I have a better idea. We could go back to my place. I could cook for you." His fingers touch his chin in contemplation. *What am I thinking? Rick always did the cooking.* I shake that off. I am not completely incompetent in the kitchen. "I make a mean breakfast." He smirks. I palm my face. "That's not what I meant."

"Uhuh. Are you trying to seduce me Miss Thornbush?" *Is it warm in here?* My cheeks are on fire. The blush on my face causes him to chuckle. "I didn't mean to embarrass you. I'm kidding. I'd love to have breakfast for dinner... or any other time you're offering," he says with a wink.

"Let's just start with dinner," I say, breathy. Though, my mind is now picturing waking up, wrapped around him.

"It's a date." Blake fumbles with some folders on his desk. "I just have a few loose ends to tie up, and we can get going. I'm going to pop into Ben's office. Okay?"

"Sounds good." While he's going over any last-minute items with his partner, my mind visualizes my pantry. I don't normally have a ton of food at home, being single. There's wine, that's a start. Anything else, I can wing it... I hope. All else fails, I have the box from Scents and Bake Ability.

We walk to the parking garage, his hand on the small of my back. His sleek black car is sporty, with a side of luxury. Definitely a man's ride. Like his suit the first time we met, it was tailor-made for him. Blake opens the door, and I sink into the softened leather. After tossing his jacket to the back, he takes his seat behind the wheel, the sound of the motor purring excites me. This thing has some horses under its hood. Putting it in reverse, he backs out, shifting into first gear. Yeah, it's a stick. There is just something sexy about shifting gears. Once we get out of the city, he really cuts loose, and lets it fly. His footwork going from clutch to gas, clutch to gas. The muscle in his arm flexing as he shifts higher and higher. It's so freaking hot.

I look down to find his hand on my thigh. When did that happen? He's smooth, I'll give him that. The radio plays some random pop song. It takes me back to my teen years, and school dances. Not the formal ones. The ones where you just go with your girls, dancing the night away. Your greatest wish, that the cool boy from class tells his friend, to tell your friend, he likes you. That kind of song. We look at each other and laugh. Maybe we both have the same thought. The next thing you know, the two of us are singing, off-key, at the top of our lungs. Cue every rom-com moment in time. This makes me smile.

"What? Is my singing that bad?" he asks.

"No. Just writer brain. Happens all the time."

"So, are you picturing me in your next great novel?" Now, that makes me laugh.

"Let's just say, you made the novel the moment I met you."

He cringes. "You killed me off, didn't you? I was such an ass." I shrug, then look at him with guilt. "Oh my God, you DID kill me off!" Blake says.

"Let's just say, it went from contemporary woman's fiction to suspense thriller, really quick."

"I deserve that."

At my home, he is surprised how "in the country" it am. Yes, I am not an extremely far distance from the city, but it has the feel of it. I love it here. It is my home, my refuge. Autumn is in full force with its landscape of colors. Trees lined the drive to my two-story farmhouse. My favorite spot, the huge, inviting porch with the coziest swing you could imagine. It is deep, covered in pillows that match the season. Burgundy, gold, and brown colored fabrics and patterns. A soft, blanket decorated with leaves and pumpkins drapes across the seat. Even now, I want to put on some comfy leggings and over-sized shirt, curl my socked feet up under me, sip my wine, and swing.

That thought will have to wait. I promised this man some food. What was I thinking? He follows me up onto the porch. I smile when I see him eying the swing. I open the door and Cecily bolts between my legs to greet me, practically tripping me. I scoop up the fluffy Mainecoon cat. She buries her head in my neck and purrs. I introduce Blake to Cecily. She must like his petting. The cat pushes her head into his hand. Love at first sight. I set her down to go to the kitchen, and she circles his feet.

He stumbles, trying not to step on her, grabs me on the way down. Luckily, we fall into a nearby loveseat... how appropriate.

He hovers above me, staring into my eyes. I see mischief in them. That, and a longing. I lick my lips; his gaze follows the movement. Closer and closer, his lips get. I lift my head to meet him halfway. My eyes close. His hand cups my cheek. The pillowy lips meet mine. Soft and gentle at first. I feel the scruff of his beard on my face. He deepens the kiss; and I am all in. Blake's tongue gently swipes my lips, and they part for him. Our tongues now tease and tempt each other, I melt into it. I had imagined for a long time now, how he kissed. Even in my wildest imagination, I never pictured it this amazing. You can tell when someone enjoys kissing. We lost track of time. It didn't exist in this world we created. Nothing exists, but myself, and this handsome man above me.

Things heat up as we make ourselves more comfortable. Hands are free to roam, to explore. I expected his hands to be soft. Businessman, computers, office work. They weren't rough, like someone who made his living working them hard. They weren't soft either. It had me perplexed. What did this man do in his spare time? Obviously, he isn't scared of manual labor. I am intrigued and want to know more about him. That is going to wait until... yes, that's the spot. What was I thinking about?

CHAPTER TEN

Nila Thornbush has got to be the sexiest woman on the planet. How could I possibly not see that the first time I met her? I really was such an ass. I vow to do everything in my power to make it up to her. Once inside, she introduces me to the biggest damn cat I've ever seen outside of the zoo. At least, this beast seems to like me. That is, until she put it down. Now it's circling me. It may or may not be close to pouncing. Spinning, the long fur sticks to my pants. I try to follow Nila to the kitchen while avoiding stepping on her pet. The next thing I know, I'm falling. I grab the first thing I could to steady myself, her. We both fall onto her cornflower blue and white checked loveseat.

All I can think about it kissing her, and stripping her clothes off of her. Those dazzling eyes, those coral lips, my wanting her evident. My gazes meets hers, looking for a hint that she wants this as much as I do. She licks her luscious lips. I lean into her, and she does the same. Her light purple lids close. That's exactly what I was waiting for. Cupping her cheek, I lean in to kiss her softly. It is even better than I had imagined. Her lips part for my teasing tongue, and I feel my pants tighten with the arousal. We kiss for who knows how long. Time is irrelevant. My hands seek contact with her skin, as I slide them under her shirt. Her breath hitches when my thumb grazes her nipple over the thin bra. I need more of her. Unbuttoning her shirt, my lips trail across each new part of exposed flesh. Slowly, I take it off, and start to work on that sexy, lace bra next.

Gasping for breath, she stops me. "Bedroom?" is all she manages. I'm to my feet in seconds, lifting her into my arms. Her legs and arms wrap around me, lips crushing mine. It's not an easy feat to feverishly kiss, all while trying to maneuver around an unfamiliar place, but I couldn't stop kissing her. She tastes sweet, the icing from earlier on her tongue.

"Which way?" I ask desperately, while carrying her. She motions down the hall, and hungrily kisses me. I'm trying to kiss her back, carry her, watch out for that furry mammoth, and get her to bed before she changes her mind. I'm not worthy of this incredible woman, and I need to be inside her. Lying her on the bed, she unzips and shimmy's out of her skirt. Her bra and lace thong are her only clothing now.

Nila leans up to get me out of my own clothes as quickly as possible. Her gasp at my now free length makes me chuckle. She gives me a wicked grin before wrapping her hand around it. She begins stroking me before sinking those lips over my hard cock. I throw my head back in pleasure. My fingers work to free her her hair from the clip. Long waves spill down, and I wrap them around my fist. Giving it a gentle tug for her to release me, she obliges. As amazing as her mouth feels on me, I need to taste her, worship her, then be inside of her.

Easily lifting her, I push her further back onto the bed. I take a pillow, and tuck it under her so that her hips are tilted. Rising above her, I kiss her lips, then work my way lower, and lower down her body. She giggles when I get to a certain part of her stomach. I mentally tuck away that little tidbit for another time. With her legs open for me, I gaze down, then meet her eyes. "I bet it tastes as good as it looks." With that, I bury a finger inside, her wetness coating it. I pump it a few times before pulling it out and placing my finger in my mouth. "Mmm, even better." Nila groans. My tongue, now tasting her, licking her, slowly at first, then I pick up the tempo.

The palm I have placed on her stomach feels her body tighten, her breath catches and holds. She's close, so I keep doing the exact same thing that got her to the edge.

She moans loudly as she lets herself go, giving into the pleasure. When I don't stop, her body jerks and thrashes. "Please, Blake! I need you inside me! Please!" Her wish is my command. I make quick work of the condom, and slowly enter her. I let her get accustomed to my size. She's so tight around me. My thrusts increase, I'm no longer in control. The feeling is ecstasy. I pull her into a seated position above me, her legs wrapped around my torso. Arms around her, I swiftly raise and lower her onto my shaft. She throws her head back as she rides me. When she leans forward, Nila gives a devilish grin, and pushes my body so that my back is now on the bed. Repositioning, she rises and lowers on me with fury. My hands grip her hips, and we come together.

Our bodies covered in sweat, we collapse together, me still inside her. I kiss her again, never wanting this to end. "I don't know about you, but I'm dying of thirst. And starving," I say.

"Same. You wanna grab some snacks and water, then come back here, or do you want me to cook?" she asks.

"Such a decision." I flip her over and hover above her. "I vote noshing in bed, hands down." My teeth teasingly graze her lip before kissing her.

She smiles playfully at me. "I was hoping you'd say that. Just an FYI, I'm a horrible cook."

"Why did you invite me here for dinner? We could have gone out," I answer. Or, you could have made that famous breakfast for dinner idea.

"Heat of the moment. Besides, we wouldn't have this."

"True. This is definitely worth it."

I excuse myself to dispose of the condom and clean up. As I come out, she grabs my shirt and puts it on. I give her a curious look, and she shrugs before answering. "I've always wanted to bop around the kitchen in a man's dress shirt."

"Well, by all means, bop away," I say, and motion for the door. We make our way to the kitchen in search for sustenance. We must be planning a marathon with all the goodies we haul back to bed. She's carrying several bottles of water, the condensation sliding down the side of the bottle. Once long water droplet slides down her finger. I clumsily juggle snacks from salty, to savory, to sweet. I think we are going to be here for a while, and I am completely okay with that. Back to the bed. The one you sink into. There's little firmness. It sinks and envelops you, a lush light gray comforter, is spread haphazardly across the bed. White pillows tossed here and there. It has a farmhouse theme, and can't tell she spares no expense when decorating. You can tell every item is hand-picked to go perfectly with the room and theme.

CHAPTER ELEVEN

Blake did manage to get up and head in to work this morning. Myself, well, that's the beauty of being a writer. I can work anywhere, wearing anything, or nothing. The poor guy didn't get much sleep last night. However, he did leave with a smile on his face. I pull the soft blanket up around me, grinning, and remembering the night. He is coming back after work, and picking up dinner. He really doesn't seem to care that I can't cook.

Cecily jumps on the bed and meows loudly, rubbing her furry body against mine. "Okay, okay. I'm getting up to feed you. Can I throw on some clothes first?" Her noisy reply told me that I better make it snappy. So impatient. I get dressed in leggings, and boxy shirt. Managing to get on some comfy socks before her sounds became desperate. That cat could use a diet, she is by no means starving to death. I serve the queen of the castle her food, and brew myself some coffee. The smell alone giving me a buzz. I fill my favorite mug, a gift from an author friend of mine, and load it with creamer. Picking up my laptop, I take it, and my brew with me outside to the swing.

I wrap the soft, autumn decorated blanket around me, and sip. Ah, heaven.

Looking into the yard, I notice the colors of fall around me. The shades of greens in spring and summer have given way to rich reds, golds, oranges, and browns. A breeze picks up a fallen leaf, dancing it across the blue sky. On the other side of the neighbor's fence, I watch a calf jump and play, as the mother moseys along eating the grass just over my side of the fence. I wonder if that's where the saying the grass is always greener comes from?

My neighbor, Elmer Miller, raises those Scottish Highland cows. The adorable ones with the long coats, and big horns. Sometimes, I shimmy between the fence, and just sit out there with them. Oh, he's aware that I do it. Once, I had fallen asleep out there. I woke to the older man staring down at me shaking his head. I was curled up with my head on Betty, and Barney had his head on my feet. Betty is the one that has the new calf. Yes, his name is Bam Bam. All I can say is thank goodness, it's not an electric fence.

Another sip, then I open my laptop. First, I check on the book sales of my ones that are still indie published. One thing about the televised interviews, it didn't just increase my books with Archer Quill. All of my old books have jumped in sales, too. Then, I check the book review sites, leaving reviews on them for two of the books I'd read this week. One by author Christine Michelle, and the other by author Liberty Parker. Once my five-star reviews are done, I move on to my author pages and groups, checking in. By the time I take the last sip of coffee, I'm finally done with all of the extras that need done, and can actually write. This requires another cup, and probably a Danish. Can't work on an empty stomach.

Just as I'm finishing doctoring my second cup, my phone buzzes. It's him. "Good morning. I just wanted to see how you were doing. Oh, and what do you prefer, Italian, or Chinese?"

"I'm absolutely perfect. Did you make it to work on time?" I ask.

"Yes, I'm realizing you are. And a few minutes late, but I'm the boss so..."

I blush, though he can't see me. "Chinese." Trying to not get too gooey. "I like pretty much anything, as long as it's not too spicy. As long as there is some Crab Rangoon at the end, I'm good."

He chuckles. "I'll pick up a few different things. Don't forget the crab, check. My next appointment is here, I need to go. I had a great time last night."

"Me too," I say. Probably a little to dreamily. "See you tonight."

"Looking forward to it."

My uncontrollable smile beams behind my coffee mug. My feet seemed to glide back out to the porch. *Work, Nila.* I need to start writing. I've got this. Turning sideways in the swing, I set my laptop in front of me ready to go. *Let's see. If he gets out of work at five, then takeout, the drive here, that will put him here around six thirty. He's probably going to want to change. So probably seven. I wonder if he'll bring clothes with him. Write Nila! You act like he's the first man you've ever been attracted to. It has been a long time. Oh my God, I need to stop.*

I am seriously feeling that video where the sound clip does the super-fast talking, then the kid stuttering trying for form a sentence. My mouse clicks on my latest story, and just like that, I write. I've really tried being one of those organized people with the notes and story cards. It's not in me. I'm a pantser. Always have been, probably always will be. The story just appears as my fingers hit the keys. Who knows where is takes me until I'm right there, deep in the heart of it. How it progresses and ends is just as much a mystery to me, as the reader.

Clicking away on the keyboard, I lose all track of time. The only thing that has made me take pause is my bladder. I back up my file, and look down at the time in the right corner of my computer. That can't be right. Crap! I have less than an hour to get beautiful, pick up, and tidy the bedroom, and everything else. I grab my laptop, empty mug, and rush inside. I put it on the charger, and head to the bathroom. As I hear him pull up, I'm finishing making the bed with clean sheets. Whew! I dash to the door, jumping over

Cecily like she's a hurdle, and I'm on the track team.

Deep calming breath, and I open the door casually. "Hey there. How was work? Let me take some of that." He has two huge bags of takeout, a bottle of wine, and a small duffel bag.

"I hope you don't care. I didn't get time to change after work. Any chance I could take a quick shower?" he asks.

"Moving awful quick there, Mr. Chandler. Already bringing extra clothes..." his face turns beet red. "Oh, my God. Joking. Seriously. Of course, go shower up. I'll get the food set up."

"Are you sure?" he asks, still embarrassed.

"Blake, I swear, I am just teasing." I take the food and wine from him, setting it on the table. I wrap my arms around him, giving him a welcome kiss. "Go shower, put on something more comfortable than that monkey suit. It's officially the weekend. Time to relax."

That eases him. Blake takes me in his arms and gives me another pantie dropping kiss before heading to the shower. With a kiss like that, I may join him in there. I arrange the food, giggling at the fact he got a little of everything, and extra Crab Rangoon.

The water is running in the shower. *Is he singing?* I sneak across the house like a ninja. Who knows why? I want to hear that voice better. From the other side of the door, I hear the deep vibrato voice of the man I'm quickly falling for, singing. I know that song from somewhere. When I realize, I place my hand over my mouth. I am not sure if I want to laugh or swoon. It's *Hoist the Colours from Pirates of the Caribbean.* Now all I can do is picture that sexy man dressed like a sexy pirate. I'll give that man some booty. *Oh, wait. I already did.* "All the booty for Capn' Blake! We sail at dawn!" I hoist my hairbrush in the air as a make-shift sword. "If we be o'er taken, we go on with the ship, and ride the plank."

A deep voice clears his throat behind me. I freeze. "What on earth are you doing?" I shrug, then stick out my sword/brush and point it at him, pretending to sword fight around the bedroom. He grabs a long, tapered candle, that looks more sword-like than my brush. Not fair. He catches me off guard and captures me. Toned arms wrap around me, and with ease, I'm over his shoulders. I try to pretend I'm not loving every minute of this. "I believe it's go down with the ship, not on it. Plus, you walk the plank, not ride it."

I give him a wink before saying, "I don't know about you, but going down and riding long, hard planks, sound much more fun. I'm also down for more sea shanties as the spray of the ocean beats down on your very hot body."

"Is that so? Listening in on the captain's plans will get you thrown in the brig and tied."

That piques my interest. "Shackled and tied you say? Would there be a blindfold involved?" I ask.

"Of course, I can't have you seeing where I hide my gold," he says with a smirk on his face.

"Alas, Cap'n Blake, me feels the gold in me hand, right good." I say, in my best pirate accent. My hand lowering and cupping his package under the bath towel. He takes a deep inhale.

Blake, grabs me, pulling me in close. Please, tell me you have a little pirate or wench costume. Don't let a poor pirate down. My finger shot up when I remembered. I had just pulled down my Halloween decor a couple of days ago. There are all sorts of costumes, including a wench and pirate. Not to mention, Clark and Rick had left many a costume here. I'm tossing costumes over my head, left and right. I found it. My sexy pirate wench with lots of cleavage to lock up in the bustier. Each tug of the ribbons tied through, making my breasts practically spilling out of the top, makes Blake groan in pleasure.

Let's hope he just wants to yank it right back off of me, because I don't think I could concentrate on anything else at this moment. Blake questioned me about the men's clothes, and I assured him they were cleaned before storage. Rick has never missed them. That white loose shirt, buttoned down to the promised land, the skin-tight pants. Now the boot covering, hat, and imitation sword. Damn, he is making it so hot in here.

We spend the next couple hours going down, riding the plank, and finding all the hidden secrets and treasures. Mine, I've decided, is very much into role playing. I've also noticed that blindfolds, REALLY turn me on.

CHAPTER TWELVE

Spending the weekend with Nila was phenomenal, and not just because of the sex. Her upbeat personality, her carefree attitude, it's refreshing. How many uptight people have I dated through the years? Too many. Just the fact she is enough of a goofball to play pirate around the livingroom was the coolest thing. I couldn't help but join in with her. The fact it led to some fun role playing, was just a bonus. Whoa, what a bonus.

I did the cooking, which I didn't mind. Cooking is one of my hobbies. It's just not as much fun when you're alone. It's back to my other life in a few short hours. I woke early before the sun. Taking a cup of strong coffee I brewed minutes ago out to the porch, I lean back against the pillow covered wood swing. Off in the distance I see the first glimpse of colors across the field. Lost in my thoughts, I don't hear Nila come out until the swing does its thing.

"Morning," she says, holding her own cup with two hands, a sleepy smile across her face. She tucks her feet up under her and leans up against me.

"Good morning, beautiful," I tell her. I turn my head and place a kiss against hers. We sit quietly, sipping from our cups, watching the changing of the colors of the sky as the sun rises. Neither of us wants this to end. It's too soon to make it anything more than dating. I know this. We just got back into contact. We've been apart for several weeks living our own lives. Why does my heart ache at the thought of leaving today?

"I've had the best weekend with you here," she says. "Back to reality, I guess." It's like she's reading my mind.

"Yeah, back to the grind. Thanks for helping me weed through all the prospective sellers. It's been a huge help. What time is your meeting with Clark?" I ask.

"Eleven. He's not much of a morning person," she says with a chuckle. "What about you?"

"I have to be at the office at nine. Being the boss and all, I should probably be an example."

"Might be a good idea. Especially, since you have all those new employees starting today. I'm really proud of you, making your dreams a reality," she tells me.

"Look at you, Miss RITA award nominee."

"You heard about that?" she asks, tucking a strand that fell from her messy bun behind her ear.

"I may have been checking you out on social media," I say embarrassed.

"Would you want to go to the RWA Annual Conference with me? I mean, I know you're busy with your new business. Maybe you could fly in for the black-tie event that night?" she asks.

"I would be honored. Clark is going with you, too. Right?" I ask.

"Yes, I wouldn't be where I am without all his work getting my name and books out there. I'd love for you two to meet.

Maybe we can all get together next weekend?" Nila considers.

"Sounds like a great idea. I'd love to meet the people in your life." Shoot, did that come across as too clingy? Too much? I breathe a sigh of relief when I see that big bright smile of hers.

"I'd really like that!" She wraps her arms around me and gives me a squeeze. My arms follow suit and I kiss her. The alarm on her Fitbit goes off, telling us this cozy morning is about to come to an end. We release each other and stand. "Well, I better let you get ready for work." She places a kiss on my cheek, and opens the front door. Cecily greets us loudly, ready for breakfast. I still can't get over how huge this cat is.

I change into my suit, while she reheats the breakfast I had made before the swing. There is just enough time for us to sit down and eat before I have to be on my way. Why do I feel like if I leave, things are going to be different? I kiss her like it's going to be the last time, for a long time. The way Nila kisses me in return, she feels the same.

On the way to work, I listen to an audible version of one of her earlier books. The richness of her writing and characters is amazing. No wonder she's came so far. I lose myself into the story. It's not your typical romance, or at least what I thought it would be like. My brain thought it would be girly when I downloaded it. It's nothing like that. There is drama, action, suspense, and God help me, it's got some spice. It wouldn't do me well to walk into work with a bulge in my dress pants. I take off my coat and carry it over my arm in front of me. Down boy. As the elevator opens on my floor, I'm good to go, professional as I'll ever be.

"Good morning, Mr. Chandler. Here is your itinerary for the day. Mr. Williams is in your office. The plane has just landed, and Susan is at the airport," says Kelly, my new assistant. She's very qualified, but I miss the casual atmosphere I had when it was just Ben, Susan, and I with a couple of others. I don't regret the growth of the company. I suppose I must grow with it. Today, Ben and I meet again with Hanover and Benson, the men who helped us fund our project.

"So, how was your weekend?" Ben asks with a smirk. He knew I was leaving work on Friday to spend time with Nila, possibly the night. The man had no idea it was an entire weekend.

"I can honestly say, there is no one like Nila Thornbush. She may be the one," I say with confidence.

"Wow! I've never heard you say anything like that. It's a little early, though. Don't you think?" Ben puts his hands in his pockets, and continues. "Don't get me wrong. I really like her. She is not the uptight, country club, born with a silver spoon, girl you normally seek."

"And that's been my problem. I was looking for the wrong kind of girl. Nila Thornbush is not like any of the others. Hell, she's a one-of-a-kind gem. Do you know that girl spent the weekend helping me get ready for the meeting today?"

"The weekend, you say?" Ben asks. The light-hearted tinge to his voice is obvious.

"Yes, I spent the weekend with her. Anything wrong with that?" I ask.

"Nooo. Nothing whatsoever," he answers with a chuckle. Before he can finish the interrogation, Hanover and Benson arrive, and are led to the boardroom. I'd say I am saved by their arrival, but they always make me a little nervous. Like getting sent to the principal's office. One more day, and the site is up and running. Then, I can relax a little. I just want this to be a success.

My plan was to swing by Nila's again. However, the mock run of the site showed some glitches. We ended up troubleshooting until way after midnight. I decided to just crash on the couch in my office. My dinner consisted of late-night takeout from the pizza place a few blocks away.

It's morning now, and I look disheveled in my wrinkled shirt and pants. The five-o'clock shadow didn't help either. But here we are, ready to go live. I lean over Ben's shoulder, a bead of sweat forming on my forehead. This is it. The tension in my body releases as I quickly realize we are up and running smoothly. An enormous sigh from everyone in the room is heard. We did it! We actually did it.

A cheer rings out and the sound of a champagne bottle popping. Susan fills the glasses. Ben and I each give a toast. *Dad, we really did it!* I think to myself, and look up. I hope he's looking down smiling. Man, do I want to make that man proud.

CHAPTER THIRTEEN

I haven't seen Blake in a few days. His site went live, and I know he's extremely busy with that. We've sent texts a few times a day. I've been pretty busy myself. Rick, my old roommate, and Clark's boyfriend had an accident. He broke his leg ice skating. Not to mention, his arm is in a sling. Clark had to go out of town for another client, and begged me to let Rick stay there until he got back. Of course, I'd take care of him. They are my best friends. The two of us quickly got into a routine, and things were going pretty smoothly. At least, that's what I thought.

The washing his hair and cleaning is a little more complicated. Luckily, I had a walk-in shower in the downstairs bathroom. The same one that Blake had sang in a week before. I pulled in a chair for Rick to sit on, which helped. However, we were both drenched by the time it's over. I helped him with his sweats, one leg of them cut in to shorts to accommodate the cast. He's settled in the kitchen, so I can get dried off and changed.

I towel dry my wet locks, and manage to get a brush through it. Wanting something easy, I throw on some shorts and an oversized t-shirt. It's really cold outside, but the house is extra toasty.

Starving, I whip up grilled cheese sandwiches and a can of soup. Rick wrinkles his nose, but hey, it's something I know how to make. We decide to spend the day watching old movies on the loveseat. I help him hobble over. He's trying to turn before plopping down. I get twisted around, trying to avoid the cat, causing the two of us to fall into the loveseat. Sound familiar?

Rick's trying to roll his body off of me. I'm trying to squeeze out under him, just as the doorbell rings. With some maneuvering, I get out from under him. There had been a lot of flailing going on. I stand and turn toward the door with the big window and see Blake's face. He's not happy. Looking down at my shirt that hangs longer than my shorts, it appears I'm not wearing anything under it. Then, his eyes move to the loveseat. Rick is trying to lift himself up to see who's at the door. He's shirtless. Shit! Blake's face is red with anger. He looks even more furious than our first meeting on the train. Yes, this is a level of anger I'd never seen.

"Come in. Let me explain. It's not what you're thinking," I beg.

"Funny. I've heard that line before. I just never thought I'd hear it from you." He turns to leave, and I want to chase after him. It's just too cold outside for me to even get off the porch.

"Please, Blake. You don't understand." I realize that I hadn't told him about Rick staying here while Clark was out of town. It didn't even occur to me. They are a couple. I've never seen Rick that way.

He reaches his car and opens the door. With one hand on the door, the other in his pocket, he turns to me. "You know, Nila? I really thought we had something. I thought you were different. Turns out, you're just like the rest of them." He gets in and slams the door. Rocks fling into the air as he peels away.

Uncontrollably sobbing, I whisper to the icy wind, "I thought we had something, too." My arms hug my body, cold and shattered. When I can't see his car any longer, I turn and go back in. Slowly, I shut the door, heartbroken. Rick tries to comfort me. I'm inconsolable. I've tried to call him twice, and it goes to voicemail. I've text him, too.

Nila: *It's not what you thought.*

Nila: It's just a big misunderstanding.

Nila: Please talk to me.

No responses. I put on the stupid pirate shirt that still had his scent, and cry myself to sleep. Waking the next morning, I check my phone. No missed calls, no messages, no texts. I force myself out of bed to help

Rick. He apologizes profusely. It's not his fault. If only Blake would give me the chance to explain. Clark gets back into town, and also tries to give me comfort. Then he tries the angry approach, hoping I feel something, anything, besides sorrow.

A week goes by, and it's as if we had never met. How can he just end it like this? Part of me wants to go by his office, but I refuse to cause any drama in his workplace. I won't be that girl. I won't. The stories don't come to me. At least none worth writing about. I know I shouldn't be this upset. Technically, we spent one night connecting on the train, another afternoon when I saw him on the street, and he called to me. Lastly, one incredible weekend. It's ridiculous the way I'm moping around when you think about it. We've spent less than a week total together. I have to get out of this funk.

Days had turned into a week. Then the weeks turn into a month. It's Thanksgiving tomorrow, and I'm determined to find something to be thankful for. I have my job, in a career that I adore. That's one. I have the love of my two best friends, who have invited me over for Thanksgiving dinner. That's two. My love of food and snacks has been dismal at best. Some might say I could have used losing those pounds, but dammit, I loved my curves. I'm not going to apologize for them ever, or for my voracious appetite. Screw the world. I'm going to go to Clark and Rick's home, and I'm going to enjoy myself.

I have realized that I moved onto the anger part of recovery. Reading up on the twelve steps of grief, I am sure I already had the depression part licked. That is until I saw my friends being a couple in the kitchen. Until I saw all the families together this holiday. Once I get past this part, I will soar. Right? I've just got to get past this part, and I'll be fine. Better than ever.

My mood lifts the closer it gets to Christmas. I live for this holiday. The hustle and bustle, the lights, decorations. I even join my two friends at a restaurant. We are at the bar waiting for a table. That's when I see him. Blake is out with another woman. She's stunning, her smile lights up the room as they laugh. He hasn't noticed me, and I leave before he does. It's time for me to move on with my life, just as he seems to have done. I take the last train for the night home.

When I get home, I pull out my laptop. The scenes and stories flow through my fingertips faster than I can type. It's about time. When I finally close the laptop, I'm smiling again. I stand in front of the mirror, staring at myself. "*God, I've missed you,*" I tell myself. For the first time in a very long time, I feel like Nila again.

The guys call the next day to check on me. I answer the phone cheerfully, and tell them I'll pick them up so we can get a tree. I arrive with my hair fixed, I'm wearing my favorite ugly Christmas sweater, and I'm genuinely happy. I think they're in shock. They hop in my vehicle, and we set out on our tree hunting adventure. I laugh when they try to talk me into this poor little tree with only four branches. "Nope, go big or go home," I say. That's what we did. We went huge, and we went home back to my place. The evening is a blast playing corny Christmas songs as we decorate. I am even agreeing to go on a blind date next week. Progress.

CHAPTER FOURTEEN

BLAKE

Ben had noticed a difference in me, the next day. He said something about being back to my grumpy old self. I filled him in on what happened with Nila, then reading him the messages. He told me I should at least give her the chance to explain before I wrote her off. I've been cheated on before. No explanation would make me reconsider. I saw what I saw. Her jumping off the loveseat, only wearing a t-shirt. *Probably his.* Then his head and shoulders peaking over the loveseat. The one where her and I first made out. He isn't wearing a shirt. Obviously, because she had it on. Just thinking about her betrayal made my blood boil.

My new receptionist opened the cracked door of my office the rest of the way, peering inside. "WHAT!" I bellowed back.

Her body flinched and tightened. She took two steps backwards before saying, "I'm sorry Mr. Chandler. You're call on line two has been holding. I used the intercom to let you know, but I didn't get an answer." Swiftly, she retreated and closed the door before I could reply. Again, I am an ass. No surprise there.

Every single time I thought of her, I got angry. Never would I have thought she'd bc likc the others. Never. And to think, I told Ben she was the one. I give an angry chuckle at my foolishness. The only thing going right in my life right now, is my business. It's a complete success, and it took off like a rocket. Quality work done around the globe, with happy customers leaving outstanding reviews. The more reviews, the more business. I used that as an excuse to not see my family for Thanksgiving.

When my sister arrives at Christmas time, my mood is better. I felt like I am finally over Nila, and what she'd done. My sister is only two years younger than me. Bright and beautiful, that's Miranda. Never letting me wallow, she always knew how to bring me out of a funk. "Come on! Get cleaned up, and take me out to dinner."

"You do know I can cook now, right?" I ask.

"So, I've heard. You, my dear brother, need to get out. I'm going to make that happen. Go in there, get your butt changed, and take me out. That's an order!" she says, defiantly crossing her arms. Her face, however, has a wicked grin.

"Fine! I'm going, I'm going. Just let me shower first." My sweats and filthy shirt from working out weren't going to cut it.

"Thank God! I wasn't going to say it, but you reek!" she says waving her arms, shooing the odor away.

I laugh, heading back to her. "You said you want a big bear hug?" My arms outstretched, trying to torture my little sis.

"Ew, go away! Seriously, I may gag," she says. Then, for effect, she holds her nose and pretends like she's going to hurl. Just to be mean, I pull off my sweaty shirt and throw it in her direction. Direct hit!

Before she can get even, I dash to my bedroom and shut the door. After the quick shower, I throw on something decent, and we are on our way. She pulls up a place on her phone, telling me she wants to check it out. Far be it from me to deny my sister anything. I truly miss not having her live closer. When we arrive and go in, I help her get her coat off. She gives me some smart-aleck comment, and a teasing grin. I, of course, have a come-back ready. We laugh and joke the entire evening. It's the first time, in a long time, I've been able to smile, to laugh, and joke.

Miranda has decided to stay with me until after Christmas, and I'm thrilled. I keep leaving the newspaper laying around, with all sorts of apartments circled in red. Hopefully, she takes the hint.

It's Christmas Eve, and I make a run to the liquor store around the corner for a couple of bottles of wine. I've left Ben and Miranda back at my place, with my gourmet meal almost ready. Ben is catching an early morning flight to visit his own family, but I wanted to celebrate with my two favorite people before he did. That's when I spot him. The shirtless guy from Nila's house that day. His face is forever implanted in my brain. He's taller than I imagined. Good looking. Way more than myself. He is on crutches. If he was hurt that day, I'd never know. My mind only saw her in that shirt, and him.

Stiffening, I wait, expecting her to come around the corner, embracing him. Only, it isn't Nila, it's another man. This man looked so familiar. Where had I seen him before? *Did Nila know her man meat is bisexual? Think, damn it! Where have you seen him?* Then it clicked. Her agent! I remember seeing him that night at the restaurant. What was his name? Clark? Yes, that's it.

I rushed out of the store, my brain going through every possible scenario. Was that guy seeing Nila, and sneaking around with Clark behind her back? Were Clark and that guy always a couple? I mean, they seem like they've been together for way longer than a month or so. They have the familiarity of a couple that's been together for years. Closing the door to my apartment, I don't even remember walking to, I lean against the door, stunned. It didn't even register at first that my little sister and my best friend were tongue-wrestling on my sofa.

That's one way to bring you straight back to the present. I clear my throat. The don't stop. "Ahem." Still no coming up for air. Finally, a "DUDE! Quit macking on my sister!" got their attention. Both faces a deep shade of crimson.

"Oh, hey," my sister says, wiping her bottom lip with her fingers. "I didn't expect you to be back so soon."

"I see that. So, is this something new, or do you two randomly make out when she comes to town?" I ask. Embarrassed, they both drop their heads. The timer goes off in the kitchen, so I make my way to the oven. Miranda starts to say something, but I hold up my palm. I am so not ready for this conversation. I get all the food spread out, and Miranda has set the table.

The three of us sit down to eat, and Ben looks around for the wine. Not seeing it, he asks, "didn't you go to the liquor store?"

"About that. I didn't get any. He was there."

Ben looks at me, completely confused, then it crosses his face. "Him? Was she there with him?" I'm so glad my best friend knows exactly what I mean without explaining.

"No, but his boyfriend was," I answer.

"You're kidding me? Really?" he asks.

"What in the world are you two talking about? Who is him, and why again couldn't you get the wine?" Miranda asks.

"It's a long story. A really long story," I say. I prop my elbows on the table and bury my face in my hands.

Miranda looks to Ben now, who is more than happy to fill her in. "Okay, so your brother was an ass to a girl on a train. He then saw that girl that night. Realized he was an ass. Rode the train with her again. Fell for her. They went their separate ways, busy with work. Neither of them had the other's number. Weeks go by, and he sees her in the street. He yells for her, they reconnect, and he brings her back to the office. That's when I get to meet her, and she was amazing... and super-hot." That gets a look from my sis. "Well, she was. Anyhow, you brother ends up spending the weekend with her. Comes back saying she's the one. Blah, blah, blah, amazing. Yada, yada, so awesome, perfect girl." Miranda clamps her hands together and squeals. She's been wanting me to fall in love for years. "Blake goes over to her house to profess his love, and she's wearing only a t-shirt, with a man on the couch." Miranda gasps, clamping her hands over her mouth.

Ben grabs three beers from the fridge, handing them out. He pops the cap off of his, and takes a big drink. Miranda is squirming in her chair waiting for him to continue. "Come on, already. Give me the deets!" she demands.

"I told him to let her explain." I give him a look. "Well, I did! He didn't listen. Cut to tonight. Apparently, the man in the liquor store was him...with another man."

"You've got to be kidding me?" Miranda asks, looking towards me again.

"Nope," I answer this time. "Want to know the best part? He was with her agent, Clark. They are most definitely a couple."

"So, what does that mean? Like she snuck around on you and now he's sneaking around on her? Or like, you screwed up big time and need to find her?" Miranda asks.

"I'm going with he screwed up big time," answers Ben.

"Call her, you idiot! Right now! You can't let her get away. She's THE ONE!" my sister explains jumping from her seat.

"I can't," I say with a sigh. "I deleted her number."

Miranda throws her hands in the air in exasperation. "Seriously, dude?" She stomps over to the coat closet, and grabs our coats. "Come on! We're going over there. It's going to be a Christmas miracle worthy of all those sappy movies."

"No. We are going to sit here and eat," I say calmly. "What would I even say to her? Plus, that still doesn't explain her only having on his shirt."

Miranda flops back down to her chair in frustration. We pass the food, eating in silence, except for the occasional, "What if..."

"No."

"But what if..."

"Not happening."

"Ugh!"

Ben, a true friend, tries to change the subject. "Great meal. You're really getting good at this cooking thing."

"Thanks. I love doing it."

"You'll make someone a great husband, one day." I roll my eyes at Ben, and take back the true friend part. It only gets my sister to start up again. She's wiggling around in her seat.

I can tell that everyone is full. My friend has pushed his seat back, and Miranda is currently in the bedroom putting on her "comfy" pants. At least, that's what I thought she's doing. Out steps my sister, looking her best, coat draped over her arm.

Ben stands, gives a big, after-dinner stretch and speaks. "I'd really love to stay and see how this all pans out, but I have a plane to catch in a couple hours. Miranda, wanna walk me to my car?" I glare at him. This better be a thing, and him not being a dude trying to score with my sister. When I see how they look at each other, I breathe a sigh of relief. It would be kinda cool if my best friend fell for my sis. This might be the thing that gets her to move here. He hurts her, though, I'll kill him.

CHAPTER FIFTEEN

I found it odd that my blind date wanted to go out on Christmas Eve, but I'm not doing anything anyway. So here I am, tapping my foot, waiting at the bar, two mixed drinks in, about to order my third. That's at least one strike against him. I'm sitting at the far end of the bar, trying to wave down the bartender, when a guy walks in, waving back at me with the same amount of enthusiasm. He rushes over to me, as if he knows me. The man does have a nice smile. I apologize. "Sorry, I was trying to get the bartender's attention. He's apparently too wrapped up with the blonde," I say a little too loudly, hoping he'd turn.

"Here, I thought you were excited for our date," the man says.

"Phillip?" I ask, mortified.

"Nora, right?" he asks in return. "You can call me Phil."

"And you can call me Nila." *Should I count that as a strike two?*

"Right, sorry. Nila. My bad. Are you ready to eat?" he asks.

My mind says, *"I was ready thirty minutes ago."* My mouth speaks, "Sure. Sounds great!" The waitress leads us to our table. No chair pulling out, he just sits. So, I do the same. Our waitress gives me a knowing look. Either she's a mind-reader, or she sees it, too. Sunny, the waitress, takes our drink order, and steps away. "Phil, how do you know Clark and Rick?" I ask, while looking over the menu.

"Don't know Clark. Is that the dude with Rick?" he asks. Before I can even answer, "Oh, Clark. Yeah, we met at a wedding a few weeks ago. We were at the same table. I gave Rick my card. Sell houses if you're in the market."

"Uhm, no. I love my farmhouse," I say, pulling the basket of rolls away from him, taking one. "Do you live in the city?" I'm really trying here, already knowing this date is going nowhere. It's not his occupation. That's fine. I'm just not feeling anything. Well, other than repulsion. Sunny comes back to the table with our drinks, and asks if we ready to order.

"Yeah, we will take the Chicken Piccata, hold the capers, asparagus, and a Caesar salad. Can we get that with Italian dressing instead?" He looks at me and smiles, handing Sunny the menus. She looks at me, my mouth gaping open, then back to Phil.

"I'm sorry sir, the Caesar salad comes with Caesar dressing." She looks at me, knowing I intend on speaking up. I do not disappoint.

"He'll have that. I would like to try the creamy pumpkin risotto with goat cheese. It sounds interesting. I'll take the Caesar salad... with the Caesar dressing." I give old Phil a look, then look to her. Sunny tries to hold back a laugh, but fails.

"Are you sure you don't want just a garden salad?" He pauses and gives me a long look before continuing, "with maybe some light dressing." *Are you freaking kidding me? Did he just insinuate I needed to be on a diet? Oh, hell no!* This time, it's Sunny who's mouth is gaping open. Me, I'm just mad.

Though my cheeks are flaming right now, I look up at our waitress. "Excuse me dear. Do you think you could you bring my risotto to another table? Possibly in another room. While you're at it... can I go ahead and order that divine looking chocolate thing?" I point to the mound of chocolate lava cake with sparklers being served to the table near us.

"Really?" Phil asks crossing his arms. "You are seriously going to over-react because I hinted you could lose a few? Don't get me wrong, you're a beautiful woman, but..."

"Sir, you need to leave, NOW!" Sunny tells him, crossing her own arms, giving him a death glare.

"Both of you dames?" He pushes himself away from the table and stands. "You will never see me in this restaurant again!"

"I certainly hope not," Sunny says under her breath.

He grabs his drink and chugs it down, slamming the empty glass on the table. "And I'm not paying for this!" then storms away.

"I am so sorry," I apologize to her.

"Don't even think about it." She pauses, then looks embarrassed. "I'm sorry. Please tell me that ogre isn't your boyfriend."

"Oh, God no! Blind date," I answer.

"Whoever set you up, owes you big time."

"You can say that again."

"Do you still want the risotto and lava cake?" she asks.

"Hell, yes! Can you bring me another glass of wine, too?"

"You got it!" She starts to walk away, and turns back. "Listen, I get off in fifteen minutes. Do you care if I join you?"

"That would be great. We women gotta stick together." I hold out my hand, "I'm Nila."

Sunny shakes it. "I'll put your order in. I'll bring it out as soon as I clock out."

"Sounds good."

I shoot a text to my not-so-favorite couple, informing them of the disaster that is Phil. Rick apologizes over and over. Clark's is basically confirming he knew it wasn't a good match, and it was all Rick's idea. However, they both agreed that at some point, they will owe me. Sunny comes over with two plates of food, and a bottle of wine. Her attire has changed, no longer in black dress pants, crisp white shirt, and black apron. Now, she's wearing a festive, red dress. I give her a surprised look as she sets the plates down and takes a seat with me.

"I was going to a Christmas party after work. You got me out of it," she says, and shrugs.

"Are you sure? You don't have to hang out with me. I appreciate it, but really, I'm fine."

"I've been dying to try this stuff. Now, I have a chance. Seriously, the party is going to be full of creeps like him. You're honestly saving me," says Sunny. "To new friendships," she says, holding her wine glass out to mine. Our glasses clank, and we take a sip. The risotto is heavenly, and the new friendship is even better. I've missed having a female friend to laugh and talk with. Clark and Rick are fabulous, don't get me wrong. It's just not the same.

We spent the Christmas Eve evening comparing war dating stories, and learning about each other.

Sunny is a hoot. I haven't laughed this hard in forever. She told me about growing up in a small town in Nebraska. I told her about my neighbor's cows. Sunny told me how she sold everything, moved here to be on stage. I told her about writing. She's never read my books, but swore to check them out. When she told me about the party with the rest of the cast, I didn't feel so bad about keeping her from going. The male lead sounds as horrible as Phil, if that's possible.

We were the last ones left by the time Blake came up in conversation. I figured that is a good place to stop. No way I am going to run off the best female friend I'd made in a long time by getting all sappy. We exchanged numbers, and promised to hang out again after the holiday. What started out being a really crappy night, turned into something great. Who'd have guessed?

I took an Uber to Clark and Rick's place. We had made plans to dish about my date, and open presents in the morning. I had already dropped Cecily off earlier. She isn't too keen on the carrier, but is thrilled to have those two to spoil her for the night. That cat acts like she never gets any attention or affection ever. She's so needy. When I go inside, she's laying on her back in Rick's lap getting belly scratches. I gently pushed her off, landing on her paws onto the floor. I tossed a pillow onto his lap, laying my head down, feet hanging over the edge. Cecily gave me a look, turned her nose to the air, and pranced off like the offended queen she is.

Rick took the hint and stroked my hair. "I am so utterly sorry. Forgive me?"

"Maybe. I did end up having a good night."

"With that douche canoe? Say it ain't so!" begs Clark, who enters the room with three glasses of spiked eggnog.

"Hell to the no!" I sit up long enough to take a drink and prop my feet on Clark. "Rub, slave!" He sets his glass down and rubs my feet. That man owes me at least that. "I made a new friend."

"Replacing us already? We said we're sorry," says Rick, playfully pushing me off his lap.

"You two? Never. Her name is Sunny. She was our waitress. Ordered his slimy butt out of the restaurant."

"Ooh, I like her already. Do tell," says Clark. I rest my tired, and buzzed head back onto Rick's lap, filling them in on my night.

I must have dozed off at some point, because Cecily wakes me by pile-driving my chest, and I'm all alone on the sectional, covered with a soft throw. "Oof! Dang it, Cecily. I was having such a great dream. I suppose you're hungry." Her pitiful meow is my answer. I pet her, and roll the both of us off, then head toward the kitchen. She circles my feet as I look for her bag of kibble. I swore I brought it. Luckily, the two men in my life have an extra supply just for her visits. I scratch her head as she dives in the bowl. Her noisy purrs fill the room as I run my hand across her back and around her tail. That's her next favorite thing to food.

The smell of coffee and bacon wake my sleepy friends. They are so cute with their matching pajama bottoms, one running his fingers through his hair, the other, scratching his beard. "Merry Christmas, sleepyheads. Did I keep you up too late last night?"

Clark steals a piece of bacon from the plate, while Rick pulls down two mugs from the cabinet. "I don't know how much you drank before you got here, but two cups of eggnog, and you were out," Rick says.

"They were pretty spiked, though," adds Clark. "All we get is coffee and bacon?"

"You know I don't cook," I say, "be grateful you got that."

"I'm grateful you didn't cook," said Rick. That earned him a swat with the dishtowel in my hand. He laughed, successfully dodging it. "I've got this. Get out of here woman." I dove at him, but he held one of his crutches up, blocking my attempt. He's most definitely gained balance since he was staying at my place.

"Come on, Nila. We know where we're not wanted," Clark says, his hands on my shoulders. I lift my nose up in the air and turn to leave, just as Cecily had done last night. That earned laughter from both of them.

We ate a wonderfully prepared breakfast, not by me, and now it's time to open gifts. We are now all teary-eyed as Rick gives Clark his gift. It's an engagement ring, and memorable proposal. Of course, he says yes. I knew Rick had plans to do it, hence him wanting me to be here this morning. "I am so happy for you guys! I love you both so much!" I congratulate my two favorite people in the whole world. Seeing the love in their eyes, I hope someday to find that. I'm also seeing something else in their eyes, and decide to pack up my cat and head home. They need some alone time to celebrate their engagement. I call an Uber, giving real consideration on buying a car in the next day or two.

CHAPTER SIXTEEN

BLAKE

My sister drove me to Nila's house. I gave her directions between panicking about what I am going to say. My gut told me that Clark and that guy were always a couple, and I was an idiot. Why didn't I let her explain? Especially after all the texts and calls she made. She tried. Nila tried, and I wouldn't have any part of it. If she never forgave me, I'd understand. There isn't one part of me that would like it, but I deserved whatever karma had in store for me. "Is it hot in here? Do you have the heater on?" I ask my sister.

"Uhm, yeah, dork. It's winter, you know, like Christmas Eve," she answers, giving me a look. Her thumbs tap on the steering wheel to the beat of *Billy Squire's Christmas Song.* Then she looks back at me guiltily. "Do you know what you're going to say?" she asks softly.

"Not a clue. Any ideas?" I ask.

"Other than begging for forgiveness on your hands and knees, no."

"What do I do if she won't take me back?" I ask. I lean my head down, putting it in my hands, gripping my hair. I turn to my sister, my head still down. "What do I do, Randa?"

She places her hand on my shoulder. "You keep trying. If there is any chance that she's the one, you keep trying." I nod my head. She's right. The closer we get to Nila's house, the faster my knee bobs and taps. *She's going to forgive me. She's going to forgive me.* Over and over, I repeat in my mind, hoping if I do it enough, I'll believe it. When we pull up, all the lights are out. My heart sinks. I trudge, defeated, to her door through the fresh, fallen snow. Knock, knock, knock. I pull my coat tighter around me and wait. Nothing. My head turns back towards the car where my sister is motioning for me to keep trying. I knock again and wait. No lights, no movement. Again, I turn to Miranda. This time she gives me a shrug.

I open the door and sit back in the car. My cold hand reaches for the handle and closes it. Miranda gives me a sympathetic smile, then puts it in reverse. Through our weekend together, we talked about family.

That's how I know she wouldn't be going out of town. Other than aunts, uncles, and a bunch of cousins on both sides, she doesn't have family. She didn't have plans with any of them. I had hinted that she goes with me to visit Miranda, but after the break-up. Break-up, now that was a joke. It should be referred to as the day I ruined my life. Nila didn't want it. She tried everything to make it not happen. I was hurt, and stubborn, and didn't want to hear it. I throw my head back and groan.

"I'm sorry, Blake. I wish I could make it all better for you," Randa says. I know she would. My sister would do anything for me.

"I know," I say. The rest of the car ride is silent with me watching the snow fall out the side window.

It's Christmas Day, and I'm a pitiful excuse for a host. I should be enjoying the holiday, excited to have my sister with me.

I'm too depressed. She warms up the leftovers from last night, and does her best to try and cheer me up. She gives it a valiant effort.

"I really don't want to leave you like this," she says this afternoon. "If I don't get on the road now, I'll never make it to work tomorrow."

I give her a big hug, and kiss her cheek. "I know, sis. Be careful going home. Make sure to let me know you made it home safe."

"I will," she says and hugs me back. "I'll try and make it back for New Year's Eve. Okay?" I nod, and give her a half smile.

"Probably won't be up for celebrating. You can do that with your new boyfriend." I give her a knowing wink.

"Ben's not my boyfriend," she says with an eye roll. I give her a look. "Okay. So, he's not my boyfriend, yet. He's just super-hot and a great kisser."

I push her to the door and say, "Ugh! Don't tell me that stuff! Gross!"

"Have you seen his butt?" she asks, egging me on.

"Go! Get out of here. La, La, La, La," I say. I cover my hands over my ears for effect.

"Love you, Blake."

"Love you, too, twirp."

I sit on my couch, lonely, feeling sorry for myself. That's when it hits me. I slam my hands on the seat and raise. The train. I'll take the train all day if I have to. Everyday. Every single day until I see her and can apologize. At least, it's a far better plan than sitting here wallowing. I put on

the blue suit, the striped shirt, exactly
what I wore when we met. Hopping in my
car, I take the short drive to the train
station. I buy a ticket and wait. Eventually,
it arrives, and I take it to the city. Once
there, I buy another ticket, waiting for it to
head back. All Christmas Day I do this until
it's last run. No signs of Nila. I drive my car
home, waiting for the morning. The office
is closed until Monday. That gives me
three more days until I have to be back at
work for a short week. We decided to give
everyone a long weekend for Christmas,
and another for New Years. Happy
employees make great workers.

Miranda sends me a text around one in
the morning saying she made it home.
Now that I know she made it safe, I let
sleep take me. The night is filled with
dreams of Nila. I wake with a smile on my

face, and determination to make things right. *I will win her back. I know it.*

After day two and three of taking the train and not seeing her, I call the publisher. Of course, it's Sunday, so obviously there's no one there. I almost left a message but thought better of it. What would I say? Something lame about desperately needing to speak to her. Yeah, that would go over great the with company that gets her books out there.

It's now Monday morning, and I decide that I need to get my head on straight and act like the CEO that I am. Ben comes to my office, smiling, asking me how it went. He looks at my face, and knows the answer. He faces me, placing his hands on my shoulders. "You will see her again. You will get her back."

"When?" I ask.

"I don't know, man. What all have you tried?" he asks me. When I tell him, he gives me a disappointed look. "Is that all you've got? The great Blake Chandler only pulling a couple tricks out of his bag. You can do better than that. Hell, I wouldn't even give you a second chance. You are the brainchild of a soon to be million-dollar company. Do better, be better!" As much as I want to punch my best friend and partner in the jaw right now, he's right.

I pull out a legal pad and make a list, jotting down anything and everything, no matter how ridiculous, to do. It went from sending her treats from the sweet shop down the street to bigger, way bigger. In order to pull this off, I am going to need help. Lots and lots of help. Go big or go home, right? I jump out of my office chair, jerk open the door, and breathlessly call out to Kelly, my new assistant. "Kelly, can you get me the number to Clark... shoot, what's his last name? First, look up Nila Thornbush."

"The author?" Kelly asks.

"Yes, that one. Find out her agent's number. It's Clark something. Put me through to him asap."

"You have a meeting at two," she says.

"Cancel it." Then I call out, "Ben! I need you, man!" My best friend walks out of his office, sees my face, and grins ear to ear, rubbing his palms together.

"I can't wait to hear this. You finally have a decent plan?" he asks.

"I've got a doozy," I reply.

Ben and I lock ourselves away in the meeting room. We've got both laptops open, both phones busy making calls. I still haven't heard from Clark yet. Just as I think it, Kelly's voice appears over the speaker on the phone. "Mr. Chandler, I

have Mr. Deveroux on the phone, line
one."

"Kelly, I ..."

"Mr. Clark Deveroux, Mr. Chandler," she
interrupts. My palms are instantly sweaty.
What if he is angry, and refuses to help?
The whole plan needs him in on it.

Ben reads my hesitation, places his
hand on my shoulder. "You've got this," he
says. I nod my head, and suck in a breath.
Then, I hit line one.

CHAPTER SEVENTEEN

It's been a few days since Clark and Rick's big engagement on Christmas morning. I decided to have them over for brunch. Who am I kidding, the only one that's cooked, and I mean really cooked, in this cozy kitchen is Rick. Oh, and Blake. Man, I miss him. *Nope. Not going to go there.* I shake it off. It took forever for me to recover. I'm not falling down that hole again. The room smells of fresh brewed coffee, the good kind. Spread across the sage colored tablecloth are pastries, store-bought of course, fresh fruit, avocado toast, bacon, and eggs, that I can make like a pro. Apparently, my only forte is breakfast food. I can't make anything else to save my life. The center is filled with fresh flowers. It's beautiful, set with my grandma's antique dishes. I may not be able to cook, but I can decorate a table.

I hear the door open, and turn to my amazing friends. Both gave me a look when I told them I had made a date. I may have joined a dating site, and once I weeded through the fake accounts and scammers, met what seems to be a great guy. We've been texting and calling a lot in the last few days. Color me shocked when they told me to cancel. They are definitely acting strange. They were all fired up for me to start dating again, now they aren't. I made a date with someone for New Year's Eve, and they have me feeling like it's the biggest mistake in the world. So, I'm canceling. Right now, as a matter of fact. It's a few days from the biggest celebratory night of the year, and I'm canceling. Truthfully, I don't normally have a date for it, anyway. The three of us go out and paint the town. I just thought with them engaged now, it's time I find my own other half. So what do I tell this guy? I hate lying with a passion.

Nila: *Hi, Bill. I know we had plans to go out, but I'm going to have to cancel.*

Bill: *Is everything okay?*

Nila: *Yeah, I'm fine. Something just came up. I'm so sorry.*

Bill: *Found a better offer. I get it.*

Nila: *No, that's not it at all.*

Now, I've hurt the guy's feelings. Just great. I look over to my friends. "I swear," and point my finger at them, "you two better make this right. I think I broke his heart."

Clark rolls his eyes. "Nila, you haven't even met in person yet. I'm sure he'll get over it. Besides, I have someone better for you in mind." Rick elbows him in the ribs. "Ow!" Rick gives him a look to silence him. Now, I know something is up.

"Okay, spill it," I demand. "Please tell me that you two haven't fixed me up with another Phil. I don't think I can handle it." I look down at my phone. There is three dots, then they disappear. The wooden chair creeks as I flop down in disappointment. Cecily jumps onto my lap to comfort me. I snuggle and stroke the giant ball of fluff. "At least I have you. Don't I, sweetie?" She pushes her head into my hand, and purrs. Then, starts hacking up a hairball in my lap. I grab her and set her quickly on the floor. Oh, the joys of being a pet owner.

Rick is not phased in the least, popping a ripe strawberry in his mouth, and then grabbing the ivory China plate, embellished with flowers and gold trim. That, or he's avoiding answering me by keeping his mouth full. Clark joins him with his own plate, grabbing the avocado toast, and a pastry. I give in and join them. I'll wait until their stomachs are full, and catch them off guard.

"So, what's he like?" I ask.

"Who?" Rick says, through a bite of toast.

"The guy you're fixing me up with."

"I don't have any idea what you're talking about," Clark answers. The line between my brows wrinkle, and I give him a look. "Fine," he says with a huff. "He's good looking, works in an office." I motion with my hand for him to go on when he pauses. "I don't know, Nila. He's a man. You'll like him."

"You mean, how I liked Phil, you set me up with? What if he's a pain?" I ask.

"Can't we all be a pain, sometimes?" Rick asks, and looks at Clark in frustration. Something is definitely going on with these two. "He's nothing like Phil. I swear. Give me one more chance to show you I'm not the world's worst match maker. Please." His soft eyes plead with me.

"Okay, fine. When and where?" I ask, crossing my arms in front of me.

"New Year's Eve," Clark adds eagerly. He clasps his hands in front of him excitedly.

"Surprise, surprise," I say in return. "Where? What time?"

"Regency Plaza at eight. Oh, and don't worry. We're double dating. Well, actually, I think there will be six of us, so triple dating. Is that a thing?" Clark looks to Rick questioning. He shrugs.

"Seriously? The Regency Plaza? Is he a sheikh, or prince, or something? What do I wear? I need to go shopping." Now, I'm scrambling around the house like a chicken with its head cut off.

Clark stops me, mid circle around the room. His hands on my shoulders, looking into my eyes. "Nila, stop. Take a breath. What about that sequin Mac Duggal gown you wore to that award banquet? You were stunning, over-dressed, but stunning."

I let out a relaxed breath. "That is a great gown." Another breath. "And I already have all the accessories."

"See. Everything is fine," assures Rick.

"Besides, he already thinks you're a knock-out," says Clark. His eyes grow large as soon as it escapes his mouth. Rick's mouth drops open in shock.

"I know him? Who is it?" I ask.

He definitely let something slip out that he hadn't wanted. "You're a famous author now. Who doesn't know what you look like?" Clark says with a chuckle. *Is it me, or does that seem a little forced?*

"Is there something you two aren't telling me about this New Year's Eve date of a lifetime?" I ask, my hands on my hips.

"All I can say is," Clark leans in towards me a little more, "you'll remember it for many years to come. Good or bad."

"That's not giving me a lot of confidence in you two."

Just then, my phone tings with a text from Sunny.

Sunny: *I've got the day off. Want to hang out?*

Me: *Definitely, can you give me a couple hours?*

Sunny: *Dang! You were my excuse not to go to the gym, lol. Yeah, see you after I sweat my butt off.*

Me: *Lmao, sorry. The guys are here. Meet me at Lit Me Up? I'm going to sneak in and sign my books. Then put them back on the shelf.*

Sunny: *The new bookstore? I'm down. Just don't kill me if I buy the new B. B. Blaque book.*

Me: *Ooh, dark and edgy. Only if you let me borrow it!*

Sunny: *Deal! Well, I'm off to the gym. See you soon!*

Me: :)

"Was that cancelled guy?" Clark asks.

"No, it's Sunny. We're going to hang out."

"When do we get to meet this new friend?" Rick asks.

"I'll see when she's free next. She usually works in the evenings at the restaurant. That work for you guys? We can go out to dinner or something."

"Or I could cook. We haven't had a dinner party in a while. Clark?" Rick looks to his fiance and asks.

Clark slides his arm around his partner and gives him a kiss. "Sure. A dinner party sounds great. Next week?" Rick smiles at him, and nods. Relationship goals, right there.

CHAPTER EIGHTEEN

BLAKE

My leg shakes as I bounce my knee setting across from Ben in his office. His, much different than mine. One wall is a shrine, devoted to his athletic days. His basketball jersey in a framed case hanging on his wall, along with his baseball jersey. A custom black bookshelf built around them with sports memorabilia, including his prized baseball, signed by Jackie

Robinson. There's a football, signed by Emmitt Smith, and God forbid you touch his basketball with Michael Jordan's signature.

"Is everything set for..." I start to ask.

"Yes," Ben answers.

"And..." I begin, my foot rapidly tapping on the floor.

"Yes, everything is ready. You've talked to the train station; everyone knows the plan. This is going to be epic," he assures me.

"What if she refuses to take me back?" I worry.

"You have never tried so hard to win someone back. Come to think of it, you never tried to win anyone back. You've got this," he assures me. I let out a long, deep breath. *This better work.* I'm so grateful that Clark and Rick let me apologize, and heard me out. Now that I have them in my corner, I stand a chance.

Susan raps on the door before entering. "There you are. I checked your office. Do you have a minute?" she asks, looking to me. I stand and follow her out of Ben's office and into mine. She slowly shuts the door behind us. "This may not be the time, and probably not the place." Susan wrings her hands together and paces. I've never seen her nervous before, and it's got me worried.

"Please tell me you're not leaving us. I don't think I could handle it right now," I say.

"Oh, no. Nothing like that. You may want to have a seat," she says, and motions to the chair. I sit, and the nervous tick of my leg returns. She pulls up a chair, sitting facing me, her hand reaches up and strokes my cheek before she takes my hands in hers. "You boys are my world. I'd never leave you unless you asked. Which you may after this." She sighs before continuing. "You know, I worked side by side with your father for many years." I give a half-smile and nod, unsure where she's going with this. "We spent a lot of time together."

"I understand. You were close. He thought the world of you," I say, giving her hands a light squeeze. "We all do."

"Thank you, dear. I've always considered you as a son. I don't know if you will need it yet, but I want you to have something, just in case." Susan pulls out a ring box, and hands it to me. I tilt my head in question. "You're father had proposed to me, and I said yes."

"But... I'm confused. How did I not know about this? You were a couple?" I ask.

"We kept it very private. We wanted to tell you, but we wanted to do it in person. You were away at college, but coming home that weekend. We were going to tell you, but..." her eyes filled with tears. Tears that glistened from the midday light shining from the window. Realization hit me.

"But he died before I got home." She nodded vigorously, hiding her face with her hands, sobbing. I leaned to her, holding her tightly in my arms. "Oh, Susan. I'm so sorry." We held each other for several minutes, mourning my father.

She sniffed back the tears, and pulled back to look at me. Pulling a handkerchief from under her sleeve, she dabbed at her eyes and nose. "You're not mad at me?"

"For loving my father, and always treating me like your own? Of course, not. You started working for my dad three years after mom passed. I'm just so sorry you couldn't have made it official. I should have guessed. You took his death as bad, if not worse, than I did. I'm so sorry, Susan."

"You keep that ring. Give it to that beautiful girl I met. She's a keeper, Blake Chandler. Don't let so many years go by before you admit you love her. Life is too short. If you know she's the one, don't let another day pass before you tell her." She sniffles, then gives me a warm smile. "You go get that girl. Beg if you have to. I need to see my kids happy, and you, Miranda, and Ben are my kids. Once I have you lined out, I'll work on the other two."

"About the other two..." I give her a sheepish grin. "I have a feeling that's already in the works."

"Did they both find someone, and I didn't know it?" she asks.

"Yeah," I look to the ceiling and shake my head. "Each other. I think it's a thing." She gasps, putting her fingers to her lips. The smile that beams from her is contagious. She jumps out of her chair, heading for the door.

Before exiting, she turns. "You three have made me happier than I've been in a long time. I love you, Blake."

"Love you, too, Susan." She's one step out the door when I call back to her, laughter in my voice. "Does that mean I can call you mom?"

I have never seen that woman whip around so fast and run back. Her hands are waving in front of her to keep herself from tearing up again. She throws her arms around me. When we pull apart, both her hands are cupping my cheek. "You've made and old woman's life. You better not be joking around with me."

"Never," I tell her. With one more kiss to my cheek, she dashes out. I'm sure to make sure Ben's head and heart are all about Miranda. Dad and Susan were going to marry. That's probably a story I need to tell my sister. She's in town, helping me with my plans, though she spends the majority of the time at Ben's. I give her a quick call to meet her for lunch. I twirl the two-carat diamond engagement ring around the tip of my finger while I wait for her to answer. "Hey, kiddo. Meet me at Bristol's for lunch. Have I got a story for you."

CHAPTER NINETEEN

It's New Year's Eve, and I nervously touch up my hair and makeup for about the third time. Clark and Rick should be here anytime to pick me up. What is taking them so long? I look at the phone to see if I missed a message. I had.

Clark: *So sorry, Nila. Running behind. An Uber should be there any minute to pick you up. Can you take the train into the city? We'll meet you there.*

DAMMIT! I look out the window and notice lights coming down the drive. I grab my embellished designer purse, rushing towards the door. I'm going to kill them! I dial his number on my way out the door. No answer. I look at the time on my phone. This driver is going to have to step on it, if I'm going to make the last train.

My hands are shaking, and I'm fidgeting in the back seat. I fumble through my purse, then check the time again on my phone as I glance out the window. Random fireworks appear in the dark sky. *Someone's getting to celebrate,* I think to myself. I try and call Rick this time. Still no answer. *What the hell?* We pull up to the station, and I hop out, careful not to twist my ankle in these heels, or rip my gown. That would be my luck right now. I make it to the window, just as the person behind it is shutting it. *No, no, no!*

"Please, wait! I need to get on that train." The shutting window stops halfway. I hold in a breath. Waiting for it to move one way or the other. "Please..." I say softly. Slowly, it raises, a kind looking woman on the other side.

"You're cutting it pretty close there, young lady," she says.

"I know. I'm so sorry." I give her a pleading look, and my money. Luckily, she takes it and hands me a ticket.

"Last call for 304. Last call," I hear.

I take the ticket, and dash to the train. "Wait! I'm coming! Wait for me!" My hands flailing in the air, waving frantically. Probably not something you see every day in a gold, sequined gown. A silver-haired man in a uniform, holds his hand for leverage as I board. I look down the full rows of seats, and hear the train whistle, and the engine roar to life. I grab a bar to steady myself, as I look farther and farther back for an empty seat. Carefully, I walk down the aisle, smiling at the faces, smiling back at me. Maybe because it's the night of celebrations, but people sure are a lot friendlier than normal. I'm halfway down the aisle when I see a well-dressed man stand. Relief hits me, he's offering me a seat. As I get closer, I see who it is. Blake. I shake my head. *No, it can't be. I can't do this. Not tonight.*

I turn to walk away. Surely someone will squeeze over up front. That's when things get even more crazy. Two people stand up and block my way. I cock my head and look at them. "Excuse me, can you let me through?" They both shake their heads no. Then, the voices of several passengers start singing. The two in front of me start dancing. *What is this?* More and more passengers get involved. Oh my God, it's a flash mob! I listen to the song. It's a remixed version of *I'm Sorry, Don't Leave Me by Slander.* I listen to the words they're singing as I look at Blake. He's slowly walking towards me. I look at him, then the passengers. My friends are on the train. Rick, Clark, even Susan and Sunny, Ben, and for the love of all holy, the woman I saw with Blake that night in the restaurant. She's holding Ben's hand, her head on his shoulder smiling at me.

"Uhm, what's going on?" I look to Blake, then Clark and Rick. The singing ends, Blake holds his hand out to me. I don't take it.

"I'm sorry, Nila. I'm an idiot. I was when you first met me," he looks down at his shoes. "I guess, I still am. I should have given you a chance to explain. I was just so jealous when I saw that guy." He looks to Rick. "I mean, Clark's boyfriend."

"Fiancé!" Clark yells, holding his and Rick's hands in the air. Laughter fills the cab of the train.

"Right. Fiancé. Listen, I miss you. I screwed up. Please forgive me because I'm nothing without you. I can't promise you I won't screw up again. But I do promise to never run away. Please, don't leave me. I'm so, so, sorry, Nila. I love you."

"You love me?" I say, my hand now resting across my heart.

"I love you Nila Thornbush. Take me back." He gets down on his knees. Right there in the aisle of the train, wearing a tux, hands begging.

"Get up from there. You're ruining your pants." I reach to pull him up.

"No. I'm not getting up until you forgive me," he says.

"You may be down there a while," I say. Then, my lips turn up into a smile. "Get up, already. Quick, before they start singing again." And they do. Softer this time.

"Nila Thornbush. I know we haven't had a lot of time actually together, but I know what my heart says. A very wise woman once told me, to go after love. Don't wait until it's too late." Blake glances towards Susan, then back up at me. He reaches in his pocket, and pulls out a box. He's still knelt down in the aisle. The singing gets a little louder. It's *Marry Me by Jason Derulo.* A tear streams down my cheek, and I brush it away. I nod my head yes. Cheers erupt from my friends.

Blake holds up his hand to the crowd. It quiets immediately. "Tell me. I need to hear you say it. Say yes."

"It's crazy, insane even, but yes. Yes, I'll marry you, Blake Chandler!" My body slams to his, and he kisses my lips. He then pulls back, and places the ring on my finger. And the crowd goes wild! The only thing is, I barely notice them, because I'm too busy kissing Blake.

Apparently, the train had stopped, because when I break away from the kiss. The flash mob is gone, now only family and friends. I blush and look at the ones left.

"It's about time you came up for air! Geez! Now, get over here and show me that ring!" says Clark anxiously. We are bombarded by the well-wishers. The mystery woman, turning out to be Blake's sister, Miranda. Who is apparently dating Ben, his best friend, and partner.

As we step off the train, the sky is exploding with color. A grand display of fireworks, loud booms, and hisses filling the starless sky. It has officially struck midnight, the most magical night of my life. My friends weren't kidding when they said it would be a night I would remember. Years of writing about it, and I finally get my own happily-ever-after.

Epilogue

Seeing Blake, him proposing, all my friends, not to mention, a flash mob, and fireworks. I didn't think this night could get any better. But it did. When Blake extended his hand for me to exit the limo, we were at the steps of the Regency Plaza. The most beautiful architecture in the city. Carefully, so I wouldn't fall, he led me up the concrete steps to the building. We stood on the top landing, where I looked down at everyone at the bottom. Why didn't they follow us up? A crowd starts to gather at the bottom. They look familiar, too familiar.

The singing starts up again. I strain my ears to hear them from the bottom. Turning, I look to Blake. "What are you up to now?" I ask smiling.

"I know I'm kind of pushing it. Stop me if it's too much. I have a dress in there, flowers, the whole works. Every friend and family member Rick and Grant could get, they're all inside. Marry me tonight. Right now."

"Inside? Right now? Like my parents, aunts, uncles, everyone?" I crack open the door, and take a peak. There are flowers EVERYWHERE! Guests seated. I can't see up front to know if my family is really in there, but there are a lot of people. I place my hand on my hip, and give him a look. "Pretty confident I'd take you back there, bub. What if I would have said no?"

He shrugged. "It's a chance I had to take. You are worth the risk." He puts his hands in his pockets, and rocks on his heals. "So, what do you say, Nila?" Everyone was up the steps, and by our sides, awaiting my decision with bated breath.

"Well, let me see. No planning, you've done all the work for me. No stressing at all. I just have to say yes." He nods.

Just for good measure, I take another peak through the door. Someone in the crowd yells, "Marry him already!" It was Clark, I'd know that voice anywhere.

"FINE!" I yell back.

"Fine? You said fine. So, we're really do this?" I smile at my future everything.

"Let's do this!" I answer. He sweeps me up and spins me. Blake's kiss tastes like forever, and it's my favorite flavor.

It's absolutely crazy, insane. I know this. But I plan on spending the rest of my

life finding out how incredibly not-crazy
this is.

The End